Philip Woolf

Who is Guilty

A novel

Philip Woolf

Who is Guilty
A novel

ISBN/EAN: 9783337045357

Printed in Europe, USA, Canada, Australia, Japan

Cover: Foto ©Andreas Hilbeck / pixelio.de

More available books at **www.hansebooks.com**

BY

PHILIP WOOLF, M.D.

———

CASSELL & COMPANY, Limited

739 & 741 Broadway, New York

Press of W. L. Mershon & Co.,

Rahway, N . J.

CONTENTS.

CHAPTER I.

CHAPTER IX.

WHO IS GUILTY ?

CHAPTER I.

THE STORM.

L ESBIA VILLA, where the mutilated body
was found, is in Cypressville, and Cypressville is a fashionable summer retreat within a few
miles of a great city.

* * * * *

It was a pleasant morning in early autumn ; a
gray, gusty morning with filmy clouds speeding
across the gloomy sky. The distant hills and the
ocean were enveloped in a trail of mist which, in
the hollows of the woods, was changed to a thick
fog. The invigorating, blustering wind, blowing
inward from the ocean, was plowing furrows
through the mist, tearing it into shreds, and tossing
it in the air as invisible vapor. The trees quivered
in wild ecstasy, regardless of the fact that their
leaves were changing color, and that each wind-
puff whirled about their dead companions in a
wild, Macabre dance. A pleasant morning ; notwithstanding its threats of rain and its premature

chilliness, especially pleasant to two persons who stood on the lawn before the large and quaint Queen Anne house, known throughout Cypressville as "Woodbine Cottage". It was in the days before lawn-tennis had become a fashion, and the man and the woman were concealing their deeper feelings under the mask of the useful but unexciting croquet.

The woman was young and pretty, with unusually bright eyes, and with a certain wildness in her gayety suggesting an intensely nervous disposition. She was, seemingly, indifferent to the game, or she had not full control of her arms, for she struck her ball recklessly and always sent it wide of the mark.

The man was tall and strongly built. His eyes were blue with a mild, amiable light in them. An elaborate blonde mustache and side whiskers ornamented his face, and his manners and actions suggested those of a soldier. He was, in fact, Captain Travers of the British army, on a furlough for the purpose of restoring the health that he had lost in India. He had been introduced to the inmates of the cottage several weeks before by his friend Doctor Dubois, and in the cottage he had remained an honored guest ever since. The covert, tender glances that he cast at his companion indicated that the athletic warrior was in love.

An unusually bad shot of the young lady loosened his tongue.

"Really, Miss Gower, you are not well this

morning," he said with great solicitude. "You are awfully nervous and your face has lost all its smiles. I hope that the letter you received a while ago didn't contain bad news ! "

"It was a common-place enough letter, Captain Travers," she answered with a forced smile. "But I am *not* well this morning, and I fear I shall not be able to accompany you in the visit to our friends as I intended."

"Then I won't go either ! "

"But you must," she said firmly. "We have been accused of selfishly keeping you and Doctor Dubois to ourselves. The open-air party was given on your account."

"It's a beastly day, Miss Gower, and the end of the season, and I prefer to remain here."

"You must obey me, sir," she answered with a light laugh that ended in a sigh. "I will retire to my own room and try to forget my headache in sleep."

"You do look awfully pale," said the sympathetic captain. "Hadn't you better see the doctor ? "

She started and shivered.

"Any thing but that ! " she said wildly. "I mean," she explained with a forced smile, "I have a horror of being regarded as an invalid."

"But if I must go, I should like to hear the doctor's opinion. See, he is coming down the steps now ! "

"And I refuse his prescription in advance," she

said hastily, throwing down her mallet. "Good
morning, Captain Travers, and I hope you will
have a very pleasant time."

With the words she waved him a farewell, and
with a whispered "God bless you", disappeared in
a direction opposite that in which the doctor was
coming.

The doctor was small as to height, hardly touching the rule at five feet three inches. He was
forty-five years of age, but was prematurely bald,
and the coarse, gray hair that fringed his skull was
as rigid as steel wire. His cheeks were closely
shaven, but a wiry, gray mustache curved upward
under his eagle nose and overshadowed a large
mouth ornamented with the whitest and strongest of
teeth. Shaggy, coarse eyebrows projected over a
pair of bright, penetrating gray eyes, and marked
the base of a high, narrow forehead. It was a
ruddy, smiling, intelligent face, indented with the
furrows of thought, and winning the admiration it
deserved. For Doctor Dubois was a world-famous
man, an honored member of all the important
scientific societies foreign and native, with a multi-
tude of distinguished friends, hosts of grateful
patients ; vain, tender-hearted ; a great admirer of
women, and fully appreciating his own talents. He
was dressed in a suit of formal black, and his one
eccentricity was revealed in a narrow, blood-red
necktie that encircled his neck.

He approached the captain, watch in hand. "It's
ten o'clock, Travers, and time to be off."

" Miss Gower has refused to come ! "

" That is no excuse for you ! Mr. Morris has refused to come ; that is no excuse for me. You are going and I am going," he said authoritatively, " and we intend to smoke a cigar on the way. Light up and cheer up."

" She has changed awfully of late," sighed the disconsolate captain. " I once thought I had a chance, but I'm afraid I must give it up. The bloom has faded from her cheeks, and all her energy has changed into nervousness."

" I will listen to you as we walk, Travers. We must not lose time. Come ! "

They walked over the sloping lawn, and emerged into a quiet little lane overarched by trees.

" What was her excuse for not coming ? " asked the doctor, after a pause.

" A headache."

" Morris was more honest. The truth is, that the people we are going to see are unexpectedly honored with the visit of a man whom Morris and his niece dislike. Why, I don't know or care. This man is a Mr. Hugo Addison, who returned from a long pleasure voyage in his yacht, after he and his yacht were supposed to have been swallowed up in the waves. This individual is to be a guest of our friends ; I believe he has even the intention of giving us all a little trip in his yacht. Be this so or not, he is the real cause why Morris and his niece do not accompany us, although I am ordered to give a more diplomatic excuse for their absence."

" But she is really ill, doctor."

" She will recover ! " was the dry answer.

" Poor little thing ; it worries me awfully ! "

" You will recover, too ! See here, Travers, I can only spare myself a few days' vacation. Let me beg of you not to overwhelm me with your confidence until we return to the city."

The captain accepted the hint and remained silent ; but he thought only the more. He walked onward with a shadow on his face and gloom in his heart.

They both received a very hearty welcome at their journey's end from the jovial Mr. Tenterden and his guests, who, despite the theatening weather, were also engaged in the unstimulating game of croquet, and gay words and gayer laughter defied clouds and piping winds.

The women of the party had thrown shawls or wraps over their shoulders on emerging from the house ; but as their blood became warmed by exercise these were carelessly thrown aside or sentimentally carried by happy cavaliers.

The natural joy of hearty youth was increased by the knowledge that the season was nearly at an end, and that in a few days, the great dusty city would absorb these pilgrims of summer and fashion, and the little village be surrendered to dust, desolation and the vulgar aborigines who were neither rich nor fashionable.

The doctor avoided the tempting snares that were set for him, but the helpless captain was appropriated by a vivacious blonde with an elaborate head of red hair, and a pretty but insipid face. Miss Selina Carlyle was doubtless very attractive ; but she only wearied the moody captain.

" I really didn't expect to see you, Captain Travers. Your friends have kept you so cruelly secluded that I thought I should never see you."

" I came over here with the Indian malaria in my blood, and seclusion was what I needed."

" Yes, but they might have amused you with some company," continued the very pert young lady, " though I suppose, under the circumstances, they would find it difficult ? "

" May I ask why ? "

" Don't you really know ? " she asked, with an affectation of great surprise. " Forgive me, then ! your seclusion has been very complete. But I really fear we shall not be able to enjoy the yacht voyage after all, it does so look like rain. But I suppose you don't care ? "

" I fear, not greatly."

" But they say that Mr. Addison's yacht is such a great curiosity. He has been away a year, and he gathered odd things from all parts of the world, till I am told it is a perfect little palace. And how strange it was ; all his friends really mourned his death, supposing the newspaper report was true, and that he had been drowned, and none of us knew that he was in the land of the living, until he himself appeared with the happy news. I suppose you don't know him, Captain Travers ? "

"I have not that honor."

"Of course not. How absurd to ask! But I know you will like him; he is such a perfect gentleman! And so chivalrous! Always doing some charity or delighting his friends with some delicious little surprises. I am so glad you have come!"

"Miss Gower is ill, and at first I had no intention of coming without her."

"I didn't know she was invited!" said Miss Selina, with a little spiteful, cattish purr. "One can see that you are not curious. But do tell me about India and tigers! I perfectly dote on both!"

While the captain was suffering this martyrdom, the doctor was quietly walking about, exchanging a few pleasant words with all the pretty women, and honoring the men with an abrupt nod of the head. But his was a social, not gregarious nature; and where one or two would have amused, a greater number of chattering people only bored him; and he crept away to enjoy a cigar in solitude.

Leaving the lawn, he entered a quiet little path that led downward to the gate, where he was suddenly confronted by a gentlemanly man who had seemingly been running, for he was out of breath. A tall man, with russet-colored side whiskers and mustache ornamenting a pale, excited face.

"Pardon me," he gasped, "but can you tell me if Miss Gower is here?"

"She is at her home—Woodbine Villa!"

"I have been there; but was told that she had gone out."

"She is not here!" said the doctor, with a shrug of the shoulders.

The man paused irresolutely, then murmured, with a frown :

"It will be too late, too late!" and, turning on his heel, disappeared.

"A madman!" said the doctor quietly, puffing away the incident in a cloud of smoke.

As the morning wore away, the expected pleasure-trip became the topic of general conversation, and its liberal, agreeable owner, of general commendation. When, in the afternoon, the women retired to prepare for what promised to be a boisterous voyage, a few of the more active men descended the bluff leading to the shore, and walked out on the private dock to smoke their cigars and to watch for the expected yacht.

Among the idlers on the dock were Doctor Dubois and the wearied captain, who would have faced a score of tigers rather than again submit himself to the society of the vivacious but spiteful Miss Selina Carlyle, whose wearisome conversation had made him disgusted with the world in general and himself in particular.

There had been several light showers in the afternoon, of a few minutes' duration each, but now a heavy storm, was threatening. The doctor glanced up at the sky and while holding his hat on his head puffed vigorously at his cigar.

"A breezy day, doctor!" said the stout man standing beside him.

" Too breezy for a trip on the water, Mr. Ascham; at least for me. I shall lie in the veranda on the least windy side of the house, and leave sea-sickness to my friends."

" It would be a shame to desert us when we most need you, doctor. But, I say," he added, suddenly, turning to his friends, " look yonder, and tell me if you recognize the figure pulling away so lustily in yonder row-boat. If it isn't Tom Merton I'll eat my head ! What do you say, Ascham ? "

" I say it is Tom Merton, and it looks as if he were pulling away from some of his creditors."

" Yes ; and I am hanged if he isn't going aboard the sail-boat yonder, that has been hovering around here the entire morning. Look ! it is sailing down toward the city, and will have some of its sails ripped in its hurry to get along ! Doctor, if a body is fished up and lands at the morgue, look in its pockets, and if you discover bad cigars and lots of unpaid bills, call it Tom Merton. But, I say, isn't it a little late for Hugo ? He was to be here with his yacht at one, and it's nearly four."

" The threatening weather is holding him back, and Tom Merton is a fool to brave it. But come, doctor, let us beat a retreat before the squall reaches us."

They had hardly reached the veranda, where the women had already gathered, than a vivid flash of lightning cut a flaming zig-zag path through the black clouds, and was almost immediately followed by a loud, reverberating peal of thunder. The entire landscape was concealed under a ghastly, greenish fog, through which the forked lightning cut its way. The wind had died away, but now suddenly rose with a shriek from a new quarter, bringing with it a rain that poured down in sheeted masses to the earth.

The storm passed as suddenly as it had appeared. A bright blue sky was overhead, and a warm sunlight shone down on the soaked earth. There was a sudden cry of " Max ! " " Max ! " as a tall figure, with strongly-marked and strongly-lined features, walked up the gravel pathway and ascended the steps leading to the veranda.

The new-comer was unknown to Captain Travers, who was attracted by the characteristically firm, handsome face.

"A good leonine head that," he said, turning to the young woman near him, " with its gray mane and honest eyes. Pray, who is it ?"

" That is Mr. Hugo Addison's servant and devoted friend."

" You didn't come up through the storm, Max, surely ? "

" I obeyed orders ; which were that the yacht should reach here by a certain time. I have lost three hours from the storm."

" Is your master aboard ? "

" No, he had an appointment in the village. Last night he sent me down to the city for the yacht—it has just been scraped—he said he would meet me here."

" But we haven't caught a glimpse of him all day."

" He said he would come," repeated the old man firmly, " and come he will. Please inform him that I am waiting his orders in the yacht."

But the afternoon passed away, and still the man for whom all waited did not appear.

" This is very strange !" said the burly Mr. Ascham, consulting his watch for the twentieth time. " I think I'll drop over to Lesbia Villa to see what the matter is. Doctor, would you like a little walk ? "

" I do not object ! "

" May I also come ?" asked Captain Travers, anxious to escape from his sad thoughts.

" By all means," nodded the doctor. " Come, we shall have a pleasant little promenade at least. They tell me that Mr. Addison's house is delightfully quaint."

CHAPTER II.

IT was a large, quaint house of many gables, built on a terrace, and surrounded by many acres of rich cultivated ground. Facing the street the ground was laid out in lawns and flower-beds ; facing the narrow lane at the back was an extensive orchard and kitchen-garden. To the right, from the street, was a glass house of large dimensions, containing not only tropical plants, but fruit trees of full height, and rare shrubs that would not bear exposure to the changeable climate.

Unfortunately, evidences of neglect were everywhere : grass was growing in the pathways ; the statues on the lawn were overgrown with moss ; the basin of the marble-fountain was filled with dust and dead leaves ; windows were broken in the hot-house ; boring-beetles had eaten to the hearts of many trees, and the canker-worms were busy in defoliating many more.

The house itself defied all regularity ; numerous miniature roofs shot in all directions from the main roof ; angles and gables were everywhere, with quaint windows peeping through the woodbine and ivy ; with chimneys in impossible positions ; with

roof edges running almost to the ground, when
they should have been high in the air ; with
abruptly-ending balconies, seemingly having no
supports ; a veranda that twisted and contorted
itself like an ungraceful snake ; possibility defied,
impossibility converted into fact with the result—a
building that satisfied the utilitarian and the artist
at the same time, even if it had been planned by an
inspired madman !

" He must have employed a great many work-
men to keep the place in order," said the doctor,
pausing at the gate to admire the picturesque scene.

" He did employ a great many before he went
away.   But he has been absent a year and, as you
see, the place has suffered from a year's neglect."

" It looks lonely enough despite its attractions."

" It will soon look busy, as I am told he intends
to alter the house and improve the grounds.   At
present it *is* cheerless."

They pushed open the rusty iron gate, ascended
the broad grass-grown path, and finally paused
before a massive oak door, the rich carvings of
which had gathered additional beauties from age.

"Old ocean approaches pretty close," said the
doctor, gazing downward on a broad stretch of
water that, toward the left, was only separated
from the boundary of the estate by a narrow belt
of sand.

" He has a poet's love for the ocean," answered
Mr. Ascham, "and for books. The entire floor,
on both sides of the door, he has devoted to his

library ; and in the library we shall find him absorbed in some old book, after his long absence from them, and perfectly oblivious of the passage of time."

Mr. Ascham spoke with a surety he did not feel ; and the hand that raised the heavy knocker was slightly tremulous. The blows fell slowly and solemnly, and were heard reverberating from the many angles of the hall within. They were repeated again and again but they brought no human response.

" None but the dead would fail to hear that clatter," said the captain impatiently.

" Have a little patience, Travers," answered the doctor. " And while waiting, admire the sunset in the ocean yonder. I'll wager you never saw a prettier sight in all your travels ! "

" It *is* beautiful," said the captain, after facing the dazzling west for a few moments in silence. " By Jove ! you can see the twilight conquering the light."

Mr. Ascham was growing alarmed as well as impatient.

They left the veranda, and now stood in the pathway, looking up at the house.

" All the windows are closed, on this side at least," said the doctor. " We have had our walk for nothing ! "

The captain had left his companions and disappeared around an angle of the house. In a moment he returned, with a startled face, and the words : " There is a window open on this side, and, by Jove ! I don't like the appearance of things."

A narrow flower-bed skirted the side of the house, to which the captain drew his companions' attention. There was an open window some ten feet from the ground, and beneath this window the flowers were crushed down as if by some heavy body falling on them.

" Look there ! " exclaimed the now thoroughly excited captain, pointing to a mass of ivy that had been pulled from the wall. " What do you call that stuff on the bruised leaves, doctor ? "

" Blood ! " was the calm answer. " I am not a detective, gentlemen ; but the hand that grasped that ivy was covered with blood. It would be wiser to summon the authorities ! "

" Hang the authorities ! " said the impetuous captain. " While we are waiting for red-tape to arrive some poor fellow may die. At any rate I am going to run the risk and enter the house. I won't sneak away, fearing for the consequences, when my friend's friend may need my aid ! "

This gallant speech was gratefully acknowledged by Mr. Ascham, to whose natural feebleness of age were now added excitement and terror.

" It's easy to climb in at the open window," continued the captain, " and in I'm going."

" Don't disturb any thing within or without," whispered the cautious doctor. " If a crime has been committed, what seem trifles to us will prove of the greatest importance to others. Climb in from the other side—on the side opposite the blood marks, captain."

"All right, doctor, and here goes!"

The captain was tall of figure and strong of limb, and the window was almost within reach of his outstretched hands. He grasped the ivy with one hand, made a leap, and easily caught hold of the window sill with the other hand. In a moment he had pulled himself up and disappeared from his friends' view. In a brief space he reappeared at the window with pale, perspiring and horrified face.

"A dead body, doctor!" he gasped. "Dead and covered with blood!"

Mr. Ascham staggered at the words and caught hold of a tree trunk for support. The doctor was calm and undisturbed.

"Open the door, captain," he said quietly; "perhaps I may be of some use. The door is to your right as you are facing us; around the angle."

The doctor, drawing his trembling friend after him, passed around to the front of the house, and after much hesitancy from the inside, the oak door was finally opened.

The sun had set, and the interior of the house was dark and gloomy.

"Wait where you are, Ascham," said the doctor with authority. "You are not in a condition to come with us, and you will be of use afterward. Show me the way, captain!"

"It's right here," said the captain, pointing into

the large, dark room on the right side of the hall.
" Near the window ! "

Yes ; near the window the body of a man, with
its pale, blood-dabbled face turned upward to the
ceiling !

The doctor stooped down beside it, raised the
stiff head for a moment, gently dropped it, and then
rose to his feet.

" We are too late, captain," he said quietly.
" He has been dead some six hours, and died from
a pistol bullet in his brain ! "

" Suicide, perhaps," said the captain, conquering
his own fear in the presence of the calm doctor.

" Suicide ? Impossible ! The wound is from
behind and above. He was murdered, captain,
brutally murdered ! "

" What is to be done ? "

" We are trespassers, and must wait for the law.
Nothing can be done until the law, personified by
an intellectual coroner or deputy, puts in its appearance. We have gone so far and must now
continue to the end. Escort our helpless friend
home, and then as quickly as possible notify the
authorities. My punishment shall be to wait here
until you return."

" Your place is not here, doctor ; when the
wretched news is told them at the house, who can
say what may happen ? Besides, sir," continued
the captain, with frank cordiality, " the trouble may
not be all over, and in that case the world can
spare me better than you—"

" I thought "——

" I have been on too many battle fields to fear
that, doctor ; for the rest, I can walk up and down
here smoking my cigar."

" Perhaps your way is best."

" I *know* it is," he added firmly ; " but relieve
me as soon as possible."

The doctor nodded, and supporting the depressed Mr. Ascham, who had not opened his lips
since the fatal discovery, disappeared in the ever-
deepening twilight.

Alone, Captain Travers carefully closed the
oak door between him and the silent object in the
library, and then slowly paced up and down the
veranda, puffing out clouds of smoke, gazing out-
ward toward the east, where a serene full moon was
rising and filling earth and heaven with its soft
silver light ; yet the air was damp and, in the cool
night-breeze, was condensing into mist. Beyond
was the village, with here and there a dot of cheerful light shining through the trees, which the ever-
thickening mist was surrounding with a ghostly
halo.

Under other circumstances it might have been
interesting to watch what promised to be the clear-
est of nights resolved into a blanket of fog, through
which the moonlight quivered and was shorn of its
brightness before it touched the earth. The change
from full light to gloom was startling in its rapidity.
Seemingly but a moment before, he had seen the
outlines of the very ropes that hung from the masts

of the sleeping vessels moved up and down in the
throbbing waters. Now the vessels were invisible
and the ocean was undistinguishable from the fog
that rested on it.

It was doubtless very interesting, if other thoughts
would not obtrude themselves—especially the
thought of a warm, cozy house that was awaiting
him. He had come to it a lonely stranger but a
few weeks ago, yet it now seemed like a home to
him, and it held the one only woman whom he had
ever loved. His half-frozen blood warmed as he
busied himself with the memory, and built his air-
castles. A serious, thoughtful, shrinking woman,
who rarely smiled, whose happiness was suggestive
of tears rather than laughter ; resolute yet timid ;
with large, flashing, yet pathetic eyes that seemed
to claim the sympathy that the small lips were too
timid to ask. He loved her, and he was vain enough
to believe that the love was not all on one side ; yet
he had not ventured on open confession, for even
the slightest hint as to his feelings had stirred her
into unaccountable emotion. It seemed as if she
yearned to know what she was forbidden to hear :
as if fate had arranged that the world of her imagination were never to be converted into the world of
reality. The wave of destiny maliciously floated
her toward the shore that she was never to reach,
raising for her a gorgeous palace that was to be her
tomb !

The dead man and the living woman ! The one
was lying with a pistol-bullet in his brain, the other

was probably awaiting a living man's return in the drawing-room of a well-known house. Two days ago she was at the piano, soul and fingers engaged in a Beethoven sonata, when the dead man's name was pronounced, with the news that he had returned from a long journey. Soul and fingers ceased from their labors ; the rosy flushes died away from the soft, rounded cheeks, and a pale, haggard face was turned from the music to the bearer of the news. Again, that very morning, before the storm, the living woman had refused to meet the man that was now removed from the world and its troubles.

Remembering this—why had the memory lain latent to this very moment, and why did it start so suddenly into prominence ?—remembering this, how would she be affected when she heard that the man was dead ? Was he an old friend ; was he ?—

His reflections and promenade were both suddenly interrupted by a strange sound that seemed to come from the library. With hushed breath and cautious step, he retired into a shadowy angle near the doorway, and listened with a certain superstitious fear pervading the more dominant belief that the murderer had returned to the scene of his crime ; and yet with the stern resolution to bring him to account.

He listened ; but although all his energies were concentrated in the act—and, as a successful hunter, he had a practiced ear—he could not hear the sound repeated. " It was mere fancy ! " he muttered, " but for a moment I could have sworn it was a foot-

step.   Bah ! I am worse than a fool to expect that
they would return so long after the crime was
committed ! ''

Instinctively following the hunter's habit of concealment, he remained within the shadowy angle.
His thoughts again wandered to the old subject
which now troubled his heart and aroused his jealousy—the relationship between the living woman
and the dead man.

" Poor fellow ! " he murmured, " he is powerless
now ; but for her sake and my sake I hope she
didn't love him. It will ruin both our lives, for I will
never consent to be a second lover to my wife ! ''
He paused, listened, and then exclaimed, in wild
excitement :

"I am not mistaken this time.   Somebody is
cautiously walking in the dead man's room ! "

There could be no doubt of it—somebody was
walking over the waxed and uncarpeted floor ; the
footsteps were light, but they could be plainly
heard.

" His shoes creak like patent leather ! " said the
captain, growing more resolute as the danger
seemed lifted out of the region of supernaturalism.
" Now he is stopping ; now he is walking again ;
now he is opening a drawer ! He must have learned
the situation of things by heart, for he is working
in darkness.   I wonder if I couldn't creep around
and get a peep at him if he comes out the back
way ? "

To reach the ground it was necessary to cross a

broad band of watery moonlight, and the captain wisely hesitated.

" He isn't a fool, and he has posted companions to warn him of approaching danger. I knew it !" he exclaimed, as a soft, shrill whistle sounded in the distance. "There are two of them, at least ! Shall I venture in the dark, unknown house, or remain here?" Then he added, after a pause, " I will take advantage of the light first. I'd give a good deal if I could only peep around yonder angle. I'll stalk the devil !"

He dropped on his hands and knees, and, keeping as much as possible within the shadow, crept slowly forward. On the side toward which he was going, the veranda abruptly ended at an angle made by the projecting wall of the house, and it was fairly well protected by a climbing wistaria vine. Reaching this useful screen, the captain arose, and peeped through the leaves. From his position the side of the house was outside the line of his vision, but the narrow, curving pathway was in full view.

Standing out in bold relief was a human figure, with upturned, intent face—the face of a handsome man, with a large, russet-colored mustache and beard. The man stood in earnest expectation. Suddenly he faced about, bent his head in the attitude of listening, and then disappeared over the grass, in the direction of the conservatory. A few minutes later there was a muffled report, like that of a pistol ; but whether it came from the land or the water it was impossible to judge.

"A handsome face and manly figure for a murderer," thought the captain, "but I shall know it
again!"

He turned to his old post by the door and again
listened.   For a few minutes all was silent ; then
the sound of light footsteps was again plainly
heard.

"I wonder if I could throw myself unawares on
the other as he comes out of the room.   I have
grappled with the more dangerous Hindu thief; why
not with a native ?   It's a pity I have no weapon!"
His instincts were stronger than his reason, and
he cautiously opened the front door and crept
into the black hall-way.   He had made the same
journey once before on that very evening, and he
knew that he had only to creep into the angle on
his right to be within reach of the doorway leading
into the library.   He walked forward on tip-toe,
and had the satisfaction of reaching the angle made
by the walls, without producing any suspicious
sounds.   His satisfaction was greater as he heard
the sounds of the footsteps still within the room.

What surprised him was the boldness and indifference of the intruder.   To commit a crime is one
thing ; to visit the scene of a crime a few hours
after committing it, another.   The wretch must
have been strongly assured that his guilt would
not be discovered, to venture so boldly on the
scene !   And yet, there must have been some urgent
necessity to return ; but what could be accomplished
in the dark ? and how could he venture in the same

room, with blackness and his victim as companions?

The captain employed his hands and his brain at the same time ; he felt along the wall until he came to the opening of the doorway, across which he stretched his arms as a bar to any one coming out.

It was a bold maneuver ; but it was not pleasant, even to a brave man, to stand in utter darkness, with the expectation that any minute he was likely to come in contact with an armed murderer. Very unpleasant to imagine that his presence was suspected, and that in the room before him a pair of villainous eyes were glaring in his direction, and that the muzzle of a pistol was pointed the same way. The atmosphere around him was chill, moist and heavy, a charnal atmosphere suggesting decay ; the walls were damp, and unaccountable puffs of cold wind swept down on him from some invisible region above. Every sense was at its fullest tension ; his strained eyes saw whirling figures of their own invention, imaginary odors nauseated him, and in the intense silence his brain invented sounds for his ears to hear. But the pattering of light footsteps came nearer and nearer ; the cause passed so close to him that he could feel its warm breath stirring his beard. Evidently pausing to listen. Now they sound again, and he can hear the rustling of garments. Now! —— A yielding mass of some material is in his arms, the forehead of a warm face is pressed by the contact against his own ; there is a light exclamation of alarm uttered by a

soft voice, and he is so startled by the difference
of the reality from the expectation that his arms
unconsciously relax and the soft burden escapes
from them.   Recalled to himself, he stretches out
his hand and grasps the fleeting thing.   There is
a slight struggle, the warm flesh again escapes him,
and he finds himself alone in the darkness with a
gauzy material in his hand.

To follow the vanishing footsteps in the darkness
which they thread with such certainty, is an impossibility, and, with the beaded perspiration on his
forehead, he returns to the veranda and the mist.
What he has so strangely grasped is a woman's
silken scarf.   He gazed at it a moment with horrified eyes, then wrapped it up and thrust it in the
breast-pocket of his coat.

During his short absence the mist had turned to
fog, completely filling the hollows and spreading
out in curious spectral streaks over the water.   As
far as he could gaze he saw nothing but this
monotonous sea of mist, which blotted out the
earth and dulled the cold, blue serenity of the
heavens.   Horizontally he could barely distinguish
the outlines of objects a few feet away ; the limit
of the veranda from which he had gazed a short
time ago had vanished from sight ; the rails of the
balcony before him had also vanished, and for a
short time, in his exalted state of feelings, he felt
like the sole survivor of a shipwreck drifting aim-
lessly in a desert of waters.

" A nasty business ! " he murmured, turning his

eyes from the desolate earth to the cold heavens. " I wish I was out of it, and would give a great deal if I never had been in it. Poor devil ! " he continued, referring to the figure that had escaped from his grasp. " Perhaps she had nothing to do with the crime, and perhaps my testimony will put a rope around her innocent neck. Thank heavens, I did not see her face ! But she was dressed in some soft material that no poor person ever wore ; her skin was soft and velvety, and by the faintest sug- gestion of violet perfume in her silky hair she was no vulgar servant. If she is innocent, I hope she has received sufficient warning to vanish into space ; if guilty ! —— "

Captain Travers did not formulate the wish even in thought, but stared impatiently at the mist and prayed for relief. He had not long to wait now ; in a few minutes he heard the sound of carriage- wheels in the distance, and soon after four specks of moving light appeared in the mist, each light surrounded by a curious halo. The lights ap- proached closer and closer, and in a short time resolved themselves into bull's-eye lanterns, each one held in the hand of a policeman.

The guardians of order ascended the steps and came to rest on the veranda.

" I suppose I may go now ! " exclaimed the cap- tain eagerly.

" A carriage is at the gate and it will take you back," was the answer given by the leader of the relief party.

" Thank you, Mr. —— "

"Sergeant Oakum," was the reply, delivered with great dignity.

The captain did not wait to hear the answer, but plunged into the mist and soon reached the carriage, that received him and then sped away in the darkness. But quickly as it sped, the captain's thoughts traveled faster, adjusting themselves to the rhythmic rattle of the wheels.

" How will she receive it ? How will she receive it ? How will she receive the news of his death ? "

As the carriage stumbled over a length of stony road his thoughts drifted into other subjects ; but when it speeded along the level ground with its old rhythm, his thoughts rushed back into their old channel.

" *How will she receive it?* HOW WILL SHE RECEIVE IT ? "

CHAPTER III.

CAPTAIN TRAVERS reached Woodbine Cottage at the moment when the church-bell was striking the hour of ten. He was cordially welcomed by his amiable host, Mr. Morris, the uncle of the gentle Miss Gower ; and by his friend, the doctor.

Mr. Morris was a stout, florid-faced man of sixty, who inherited a very large fortune at a very early age and who, in consequence, enjoyed life to the full bent of his capacities. He was hospitable, charitable and obstinate ; a *bon vivant* and a self-lover. He had sailed quietly through life, carefully avoiding the disagreeable, and carefully clinging to the agreeable. He feared anxiety more than he feared gray hairs, and had a greater interest in his stomach than in the fall of dynasties. He was a comparative new-comer in·Cypressville, wherein he had built himself a most luxurious house, which was at the service of his friends, and especially of the doctor, for whom he had a warm friendship and admiration. He had never married, and, until he received his niece in his house, had maintained an uncompromising bachelor's hall, from which

every species of womankind had been sternly
excluded.

He warmly greeted the captain on his return,
but Travers was not in the mood to enjoy his liveliness. The claims of courtesy satisfied, he retired
to his own room. He was tired and wretched, but
when the doctor entered, in accordance with his
custom, to indulge in a little friendly chat
before he went to bed, his presence was a welcome
relief.

" I sent you help as soon as possible, Travers,"
said the doctor, sinking into an easy chair. " And I
have notified the authorities. The village is con-
sidered a part of the city and a city coroner attends
to it. So we were compelled to telegraph to the
city, and received an answer that a coroner and a
detective would both be forthcoming early on the
morrow."

" I do not care for this ; rather talk to me about
Miss Gower ! "

The doctor became grave.

" Are you in love with her ? " he asked.

" Deeply, irrevocably," was the frank answer,
" although I have never told her so—in words ! "

" So much the better, Travers ! You regard me
as a friend ? "

" You have saved my life ! " said the captain
gratefully.

" Then, Travers, as a friend, I should advise you
to pack your trunk and vanish into space ! "

" What do you mean ? " gasped the captain.

" I mean your love is not of the malleable kind. According to my belief, it is only fair-weather love. Of course you will not take my advice ; but having relieved my conscience, I will relieve your anxiety. Question me ? "

" Is Miss Gower really ill ? "

" You shall hear. After the interrupted game of croquet this morning, Miss Gower locked herself in her room, refusing admittance even to her maid. From ten in the morning to three in the afternoon she was invisible to human sight. At the latter hour she opened her door, asked for a glass of wine and a biscuit, and again retired. I returned here, after leaving you and telegraphing to the city, and found the household in confusion. It seems that Miss Gower maintained such resolute silence that her maid became anxious, and, with Mr. Morris's permission, forced her way into the room, only to find her mistress lying senseless on the floor, dressed and with bonnet on her head, as if she intended to take a walk. Like the most sensible of maids, she undressed her mistress and lifted her into bed. I entered about this time. The exact cause of the insensibility I could not discover, but I learned that our fair friend was accustomed to taking bromide of potassium for her very frequent nervous spells ; and in the present instance I *know* she was under the influence of opium. I roused her from her stupor—it was not dangerous !—and waited until she fell into a more natural condition. She was too weak to be subjected to a long cross-examination, and too nervous to answer my few questions with clearness."

" Are you sure—" began the excited captain.

" I am sure of nothing," said the doctor, rising. "I've given you my advice, and answered your question to the best of my knowledge."

" As a true friend, what would you advise me to do ? "

" Have I not already told you ! Get rid of your malaria and love at the same time."

" But—"

The doctor walked toward the door, then turned to say :

" The pythoness has spoken and the fire is extinguished. Good-night, Captain Travers ! "

CHAPTER IV.

A BEGINNING.

SLEEP that night was an enemy that Captain Travers could not conquer; he tossed about in his bed, occasionally falling into a condition of momentary unconsciousness, only to return to the real world with a wildly-beating heart, a perspiring body, and a vague but painful feeling of impending horror; of a whirlpool of evil that was to attract him within its dangerous circle, toss him around as a toy, and then swallow him forever.

It was a relief when the night passed away. He rose, dressed himself in the early dawn, and pulling back the window curtains, inhaled the fresh morning air in an ecstasy of delight. With equal pleasure he welcomed, later, Doctor Dubois, who had passed an excellent night, and entered his friend's room with a beaming face.

"You look haggard and pale, Travers; evidently you have not passed a pleasant night!"

"A beastly night, doctor. I've been thinking over your words, and they have been piercing me like burning arrows!"

"They were not spoken lightly!"

" That's what upsets me, doctor. I have long since learned to honor your true manhood, severe love of truth and noble principles. Only I wish you would be more explicit."

" My dear fellow, if you were in my position you would appreciate my friendship for you in speaking even as I have dared to speak. However, I have determined to put you in a way of thinking for yourself. I am to meet the coroner by the first train this morning and superintend the *post mortem*. You shall go along with me, and if what you learn adds to your sleepless nights, blame your own foolishness, and not my anxiety for your welfare."

" At least it will distract me from my horrible thoughts ? "

" You will find it more exciting and less laborious than pig-sticking, and you will be able to compare our police system with that of your own country and France. One of our best detectives has been sent up to unravel the crime. So we will drink a cup of coffee and eat a roll without disturbing our host, and then rush off to business before the village is awake."

" Have you any news of Miss Gower ? "

" Her maid, Percy, has kindly prepared a breakfast for us, and we will receive her report at our ease."

They descended to the dining-room, where a most tempting breakfast awaited them. A very attractive young woman, dressed in simple but becoming attire, greeted the captain with a respectful courtesy, and welcomed the doctor with a smile that showed the tips of her small white teeth.

"You are the good genius of the house!" exclaimed the doctor, seating himself and casting an approving glance over the table. "I see you have not even forgotten my chicken croquettes. You are thoughtful, even though at the cook's expense."

"I did not wake her, doctor, it was so early," answered the young woman, in a soft, musical voice, and with a modest blush in her cheeks. "I made them myself, and you must excuse me if they are bad!"

"They are perfect!" said the doctor with enthusiasm, after having tested them, "and the coffee has an aroma that would tempt an angel."

Miss Percy filled the doctor's cup with the tempting beverage, and then waited on the captain. During her graceful services, while not neglecting the stranger, she was particularly attentive to the doctor, anticipating his wants and meeting his hearty commendations with a grateful yet blushing face. When her services were not required, she discreetly withdrew to a distant part of the room; yet her large, soft, black eyes still rested on the doctor, and before he had time to formulate a wish she had tripped forward in anticipation of it.

A dignified, lady-like maid, as even the indifferent Captain Travers was compelled to admit, undoubtedly born to a station above that which fate had thrust on her; but if this were true, she raised the

humble situation to her height, rather than sunk to
its level.   Her hands were small, narrow and white,
and would not have disgraced the heaven-protected
aristocracy of his own land ; her tall figure was
plump and graceful, and her small lips were full
and of a delicate color that would have shamed a
pink rose.   Miss Gower must have been strongly
assured of her own charms to place them in contrast with those of her dainty maid.

The doctor was too intent on attacking the delicious food to · waste his time in conversation, but
when stomach was nearly satisfied, conscience
returned to its throne, and with an amiable glance
at the young woman, he asked :

" How is Miss Gower ? "

" She passed a quiet night, and was slumber-
ing very peacefully when I left her."

" There was no return of the nervousness ? "

" None, sir, since you left her."

" I forgot to ask you yesterday ; is Miss Gower
in the habit of falling insensible to the ground at
odd intervals ? "

" Since I have been with her, she has had three
or four attacks like the one you saw."

" May I ask how long you have been with her ? "

" About three months."

" Did she ever speak about their cause ? "

" She was very kind, friendly and considerate to
me," answered the girl, warmly, " and she trusted
in me as a friend. I can not betray her confidences
even to you, sir."

"I have no wish that you should do so. At least you may tell me whether she suspected the cause to be organic disease."

"She *knew*, doctor, that she was not troubled with any ailment, but great nervousness. At times it drives her almost insane, and if she tries to escape from the horror she only does what anybody would do under the circumstances. She is a kind, noble and self-respecting lady!"

"I suppose, then, there is no need of my seeing her before I leave?"

"She sleeps peacefully; she is in no pain, and nervousness is not so rare with woman!" Her attractive seriousness ended in a more attractive smile.

"It is unnecessary to disturb her. If you have finished, Travers, we will light a cigar and then there will be time enough to take a leisurely stroll over to the station."

"I must change this sack for a coat first," said the captain, rising. "I will be with you in a minute."

When he had retired the doctor glanced sadly at the fragments remaining on the table, as if regretting that anticipation had been greater than performance.

"May I pour out for you another cup of coffee?"

The maid was beside him, glancing down on him with questioning brows.

"I regret to say, that I can not answer your question with a 'yes'; but I thank you just the same."

The doctor was fond of the fair sex, and was a favorite with them ; and this continued attention from a pretty woman flattered the vanity which even the wisest scientist can not subdue.

"Shall you be late ? Pardon my question, but if you shall be detained beyond the dinner hour, I should be honored if you would allow me to have something ready on your return."

"I do not know at what hour I shall be allowed to return."

"It is more difficult," she returned, with a smile, and little shrug of the shoulders, "but I am obstinate, and the supper shall be ready whenever you are ready for it."

The return of Captain Travers recalled the doctor to the business before him, and in a few minutes the two men were walking briskly through the cool morning air.

It was but a short distance to the little wooden structure that was dignified with the title of "station", and it was reached in advance of the train. To kill time they walked up and down the wooden platform that was showered with the pleasant rays of the rising sun. But few words had been interchanged during the journey ; and it was not until the doctor had lighted his second cigar that he worked himself into a conversational mood.

"The croquettes were a work of art, Travers," he said, simply putting into words the idea that had occupied his thoughts since breakfast. "It requires brains, and education even, to cook properly."

" Miss Percy has undoubted talents in that direction."

" If I were a little younger," said the doctor, with a laugh, " I should imagine that I had made a very favorable impression on that young lady's heart ! Since I have been here she has been as thoughtfully attentive to me as if ——. You must supply the omitted comparison, Travers."

" She is very attractive."

" And very good," said the doctor gravely. " I am wrong even to jest on such a serious subject. She is young and unprotected, and it is unworthy of an honest man to make light of her thoughtful attentions. She is fond of reading, and I lent her a few books. She is fond of study, and I showed her the way to gain the most profit from her un-employed time. Her gratitude takes the form of warming my slippers, and preparing little delicacies for me. But I suppose you are puzzled by my seeming indifference to the poor fellow in the deserted house. I have promised the coroner my assistance—his deputy is sick—and when business comes, business will receive all my attention. While waiting—it won't be long, judging from yonder smoke—I am in the mood to forget my profession and its anxieties. And, alas ! my work will soon begin again."

A black spot in the distance, a defiant shriek of escaping steam, a metallic rattle, and in a moment a train at rest in the hollow below.

It disgorged two passengers, and had sped away

before they had reached the top of the wooden stairs that led to the station above. One of the new-comers was a stout man dressed in rusty, baggy clothes, who slowly puffed his way upward ; the other, who carried a small black case in his hand, was a tall man, dressed in a well-made but sober suit of gray, and who leaped rather than walked up the stairs. Both greeted the doctor with friendly warmth.

"Captain Travers, allow me to introduce to you Coroner Crabbe and Detective Sharpe, our future collaborators in the cause of justice and morality."

The fat coroner nodded his head, half in deference to courtesy, half in the utilitarian act of inhaling a huge pinch of snuff.

The detective raised his hat and acknowledged the introduction with a pleasant smile.

Captain Travers glanced, in surprised perplexity, at the detective, whose profession was not indicated by his appearance or manners. He had a vague consciousness of having seen the face before, but was unable to recall under what circumstances, and finally dismissed the idea as one of his many unreliable fancies.

It was a handsome face, the eyes intelligent, the mouth sensitive, yet resolute, and the shaven lower jaw firm and square. The hair was black, and a thick black mustache ornamented the upper lip. He was tall in figure, well-made, and with a suggestion of latent strength in the somewhat delicate looking limbs.

" I have brought your instrument-case with me, doctor, as you ordered."

" I never doubted your memory ! Now you must do me another favor ; I want you to take charge of my friend. He is a benighted foreigner, and I am anxious to convince him that *our* detectives are superior to the fossil products of effete monarchies."

" I am at the captain's service ! "

They left the station, the doctor and coroner leading, the other two walking more slowly behind.

" May I be critical at the start, Mr. Sharpe ? "

" At the start and always, Captain Travers."

" Was it, then, wise to leave the tragedy so long in the hands of local incompetency ? Much may be done in a long night, especially in way of escape ! "

" You are right in theory, but wrong in fact. More has been done than you imagine. The vital point just now is *not* the murderer's escape, but to discover who the murderer is. But please inform me what you know of the case. It may be of some help."

The captain explained his connection with the murder, but refrained from even hinting at his personal experiences in the old house ; and although the gauzy shawl was in his pocket, he made no mention of it.

By the time his narrative was ended they had reached the scene of the tragedy, and the detective paused to gaze at the old house that was bathed in the morning sunlight.

" A fine old building ! " he muttered. " It looks as if it had concealed many secrets in its time ! "

CHAPTER V.

A PICTURESQUE building surely; but even in the glow of the sun and with a warm sky above it, sad, chilling and desolate. The coroner, engaged in a warm political discussion with the doctor, had already disappeared. The detective followed more slowly. As he pushed open the gate and entered the grounds, a man emerged from the bushes, and raised his hand to his hat.

"Any news?"

"Nothing, except we caught a man in the grounds last night."

"He wouldn't have been there if he was concerned in the business. I'll examine him by and by. Come, captain!"

To his companion's surprise, the detective seemed acquainted with the grounds. Without a moment's hesitation he passed around to the side of the house, and paused beneath the window through which the entrance had been made on the evening before. After a thoughtful silence, devoted to a critical examination of the ground, he said:

"Let us seek for facts. I think I've already discovered a few. Please stoop down here beside me, and see if I state them correctly."

The detective was already on his knees before the narrow bed in which flowering plants were struggling for existence in the midst of a flourishing army of grasses and weeds.

"Listen, Captain Travers ; I measure this flower-bed—I suppose that was once its object—and I find it to be just four feet six inches broad. On the outer edge is a line of old-fashioned box—I believe fashion uses tiles for bordering purposes now. In the center here, is a hydrangea that was once a fine shrub, but is now dwarfed into insignificance ; beyond, against the wall, is a flourishing colony of chickweed. The hydrangea, as you see, is crushed to the ground, as if a heavy weight had fallen on it ; and to the front here, to the extent of about three feet, the box edging is dragged forward, over into the pathway. These are undoubted facts, are they not ?"

"I dare not controvert them," said the captain, with a smile.

"Good ! Now look ; to the right and to the left of the hydrangea are comparatively open spaces, where plants and weeds have died for lack of mois-ture, and light, probably ; and in these spaces are the undeniable marks of footprints ; here, here, and here are the outlines of boot or shoe heels indented deeply in the still moist earth. Now, if you please, we will go over some old ground, with you in the witness stand. When did you and the doctor start out to hunt up the dead man ?"

The captain had been busied with the problem all night, and having a short time ago told the story, had no need to search for his facts.

"The yacht was expected at one o'clock, and I remember the servant saying that the storm had detained him some three hours."

"That makes it four o'clock. Shortly afterward you started off?"

"Yes; and I *know* that we did not reach our journey's end until after six o'clock."

"Let us give our enemies the advantage by calling it six. Now, when the doctor examined the body how long did he say he had been dead?"

"Some six hours."

"A more detailed examination may alter this; that is, make the time longer not shorter. But accepting it as an approximation, we are brought to the conclusion that the murder was committed about twelve o'clock noon. Now listen; these heel marks in the dirt were made after or during the storm; they could not have entered so deeply into the hard dry soil, or if they had, the rain would have at least effaced their sharpness. If you look, carefully, you will see that the nail heads in the heel are still sharply outlined; am I right?"

"There is no question of it!"

"Therefore these marks were made in the soil after the rain had ceased. Preparing for such an emergency, I instituted inquiries in the city last night, and I learn that it began to rain here—that

is, the heavy shower you described began at ten
minutes after four and ended at about five o'clock.
Therefore these footsteps were made some four or
five hours after the murder. Am I indulging in
dangerous theory, Captain Travers?"

"In very excellent reasoning, and I suppose we
may conclude——"

"Please hear me to the end," interrupted the
detective. "The flower bed has something more
to tell. The hydrangea, as I have said, is crushed
down to earth as if a heavy weight had fallen on
it; but if you look you will discover that the
crushed-down portions are covered with mud; mud
in heavy masses; suggesting very plainly mud-cov-
ered shoes as the cause of the disaster. I therefore
conclude that the plant was also thrust down in the
soil, not before, but after the rain storm. Now look
at the ivy that runs up the house near the window.
In one place it is torn away from the wall as if
yielding to a heavy weight. Tell me, what do you
see on those exposed leaves?"

"Blood!" said the captain. "Some one with a
bleeding hand has grasped it. Doubtless the murderer himself."

"That would be the hasty conclusion of ninety-
nine sensible persons in a hundred. But consider
for a minute; the blood-stained leaves are fully
exposed; the blood lies thickly on them. If it had
been there at twelve o'clock, don't you think the
rain would have washed it away? My reputation
on it, Captain Travers, that blood was deliberately

placed there after the storm, and consequently long after the murder. ''

'' But with what object ? '' asked the puzzled captain.

''With what object but that of leading justice astray ! of distracting attention from the guilty party to the innocent ! But before coming to a conclusion on this point, we will re-enforce our argument. How tall are you ? ''

'' Five feet ten inches.''

'' Good ! now come here toward the ivy and stretch out your hand. You see it just overreaches the blood-stained leaves, by about an inch. The bleeding hand, then, you might say, belonged to a man of about your own height.''

'' It at least seems probable ! ''

'' Let us accept the conclusion for a moment, and say that the murderer was a man five feet ten inches high. Now look at the foot-prints. Could you walk in boots that gave such a small impression ? Let us test it by measurement. Please lift up your foot. Lo ! The broadest part of your heel measures two and a quarter inches ; the broadest part of the sole of your boot measures three and a quarter inches. Now, look ! '' with the words, the detective, measure in hand, was on his knees again before the flower-bed. '' The widest part of this heel impression in the mud measures one and three-quarter inches ; the widest part of this sole impression measures two and a half inches. The length of your foot is ten and a half inches ; the length of the footmark here eight and a half inches. If these impressions were made by the murderer, he had a foot that would cause even your aristocracy to envy him."

The captain did not answer, but he thought of his adventure in the deserted house, and of the tell-tale evidence that still remained hidden in the breast pocket of his coat.

" We have still one further bit of evidence, Captain Travers, in this box edging. In its neglect it has grown twelve inches high, and a man could step over it. But supposing he pushed his way through it, would he have thrust it forward in an uninterrupted line to the extent of three feet ? I leave you to your own conclusions and return to the ivy to see if there are the same footsteps at its base, although I do not expect to discover any thing definite, as the grass grows very thickly there."

The detective carefully studied the grass, and then gently parted its waving plumes with his hands. He suddenly uttered an exclamation of pleasure, as from the base of the ivy, deep down in the grass, he extracted a handkerchief matted together with blood.

" Our murderer is excessively idiotic," he muttered, carefully unfolding the handkerchief and studying it with an amused but puzzled expression in his face. He handed it to his companion, with the words : " Look in the corner, captain, and tell me what you see ?"

" The letters G. D."

" 'The letters G. D. and no mistake. The owner
of the handkerchief, if not of the blood, has for the
initials of his name the letters G. D., and if he committed the crime his idiocy deserves the punishment it will get."

" The end is nearer than you imagined, is it
not ? "

" It is different from what you imagine ; but this
handkerchief will prove an excellent clew. We
have only to discover its owner, find out who is his
enemy, and the murder will explain itself. But it
is time to enter the house now, for they are waiting for us, before they enter on their side to befog
testimony."

They ascended the steps, passed into the house,
and immediately proceeded to the library, wherein
they discovered the coroner and the doctor quietly
seated, and still engaged in their political discussion.

" You are taking it easy, as usual, coroner," said
the detective.

" Yes, I always have plenty of time when you
fellows are with me ! But I'll go now and rake up
a jury, and look around for witnesses."

" It will eat into your week's holiday, coroner."

" Yes, if I allow it ! But I think I'll form a jury
and then adjourn for a week, to gather evidence,
you know ! "

The coroner winked, while inhaling a pinch of
snuff, and then waddled out into the hall-way.

In the meantime the detective was examining the

room, which was long and broad, occupying the entire angle of the house. It had but one door leading from the hall, but as a recompense, the three sides of the square were pierced with numerous windows, between which were tall bookcases filled with books. The floor was uncarpeted and of polished oak. Under a brass chandelier hanging from the center of the painted ceiling, was a desk covered with papers, and near it, resting on a Persian rug, a curious carved revolving chair. Heavy curtains were drawn before all the windows, except the one which was open, and from before which the curtain had been drawn back. Thick dust was everywhere ; it lay on the polished floor ; it whitened the bookcases and the books, it encumbered the rich curtains in which the moths had eaten holes ; it lay on sofas, chairs and footstools. The walls were stained and streaked, and the frescoes on the ceilings had lost their color and had crumbled away in patches.

Lying on the ground, in front of but a few feet away from the window, was the dead body, dressed in sober black. The face was handsome and refined even in death ; undisturbed by suffering and with a frozen smile on its pale lips. The massive, curling brown hair was matted together by the same fluid that formed a pool just under the head.

Detective Sharpe, having finished his superficial survey of the room, kneeled down beside the rigid, supine figure.

" You have examined it again, doctor ? "

" Not thoroughly ; that will come when you are through with it. But I can answer general questions."

" What, then, if you please, is the direction of the wound ? "

" From above, running backward. My present opinion is, that he was stooping down in front of the window, let us say, picking something from the floor, when the unsuspected murderer, facing him, and just as he was rising, fired the pistol, killing him almost instantly. I shall find the ball somewhat near the occipital foramen."

" Probably hiding behind the curtain yonder. I find nothing in the pockets but this case of cigars ; and these three letters, which I will read in a minute. His valuable hunting-case watch is untouched, but there is not even a penny of money in his pockets ; nothing indicating a struggle. As you say, doctor, the death must have been instantaneous. You can have it now as soon as you wish."

" The sooner the better."

When assistance had been called and the body removed to another room, Captain Travers addressed the detective with the words :

" Facts are less abundant here than outside ! "

" No ; but they are, perhaps, more perplexing," answered the detective, without raising his eyes from the letters he was reading. " The coroner now can run his useless course as soon as he wishes. When he reaches the verdict of " died at the hands

of some person or persons unknown to the jury,"
justice will be less trammeled in its actions. In the
meantime look here!" The detective had drawn
forward the curtain covering the open window, and
pointed to a brass-curtain hook on which was a
small blue-silk bow, such as at that time ornamented the skirts of a woman's dress.

"If our murderer was a man, captain, he was
hiding behind the curtain and wore a woman's dress;
and in coming out of his hiding place left this tell-
tale ribbon on the hook! A woman was surely
in the room. Do you see the marks of her
footsteps in the dust yonder? We have pretty
well destroyed all traces here; but look toward
the upper part of the room, where we have not
walked. Here the impression of toe-point and
heel-point are so plain that they will give me the
opportunity of measuring the length of the intruder's
dainty foot. It measures eight and a half inches,
the same length as the tell-tale imprints in the soil
without."

"But I think your reasoning is wrong on this
point, detective. As a woman stands, the point of
her shoe is raised above the level of the ground."

"But my conclusion is still the same. You will
notice that the impression I measured is closer to
the book-case, the toe pointing toward it. The
toe impression is very strong, and it suggests
that the party who made it raised herself
on her tip-toes to reach one of the books in the
case. And if you will look, you will see that on a

certain shelf the books are displaced; if you will raise yourself beside me on this chair, you will find that there are impressions of finger-tips on the dusty shelves. If you are curious, captain, here is the very book that was consulted. Don't disturb the finger-marks on the top."

The detective had withdrawn from the case a compact duodecimo volume, bound in crimson cloth. It bore no title on the outside, and on opening it he discovered that it had once been a blank-book; but the pages were now filled with a close, but bold, legible writing.

"It is a memorandum-book, and here, where it so suspiciously gapes open without an exploring finger turning the leaves, a large number of pages have been torn out. Were they compromising to our intruder? And if they were so, was that the only reason why she paid a visit to this deserted library? I will confiscate the book and study it at my leisure."

The detective thrust the volume into his pocket, and then stood gazing thoughtfully out the window.

"Were the letters that you discovered on the dead man of any importance, Detective Sharpe?"

"One of them adds the complicating element of which I spoke a little while ago. It is from the Tom Merton whom you saw in the row-boat, and it is, seemingly, in answer to one written by the dead man. You shall judge for yourself."

The detective unfolded one of the letters that he held in his hand and read:

" My Dear Hugo : —

" Your foreign trip has puffed you up ! If I borrowed money of you I intended to repay it. I'm hard up and will meet you at the appointed hour at Lesbia Villa. Don't keep me waiting and don't disappoint me.   Tom Merton."

" The envelope shows that the letter was posted in the city on the 12th—the day before yesterday. Tom Merton will need looking up. Just now we will interview the interloper found in the orchard."

The detective gave his order, and in a few minutes a disreputable, ragged tramp was thrust into the room by an unsympathetic policeman. Detective Sharpe eyed the wretch for a few moments in silence, then said :

"Answer my questions, if you can, without lying. Your name ? "

· " Ralph Price."

" What were you doing in the orchard ? "

· " Eatin' the apples wot nobody claimed."

" At what time ? "

" May be 'tween four and six."

" What did you see ?   Tell me all."

" I see a woman pass out on the balcony, and popped in agin' like a jack-in-the-box. She was dressed in a whitey yaller dress, and a white thing was wrapped around her head so I couldn't see her face.   I went ter work on the apples, forgettin' all 'bout her, and the next I saw of her, she was jist outside the walls of the place, runnin' quick, scared like.   She'd left her shawl behind her.   Leastways it wasn't on her shoulders, but her face was still covered."

"You couldn't see the front of the house from the tree ?"

" No ! "

"What else did you see ? "

" Nothin', and I didn't know nothin' till the 'cops' catched me as I was comin' out the gate."

" You didn't go in the house yourself ? "

"What fur ? I ain't reached hookin' gas-pipes yet."

" 'Take him away and keep him in charge till I'm ready to dispose of him," said the detective, turning to his subordinate. " I shall want to question him more closely by and by."

" Do you imagine he invented the story of the woman ? " asked the captain, when the tramp was removed, and with a certain tinge of remorse at his own silence.

" There is an undoubted element of truth in the statement, and when I explore the house I shall probably discover the shawl of which he speaks. But it is necessary, before I go further, that we should learn the result of the *post mortem*. The evidence will complete what I call the circumference of the circle. It is my habit to accumulate a mass of facts, before I work on the inner history of a crime. It saves time and prevents premature conclusions."

The smiling face of Doctor Dubois appeared in

the door, and, a moment after, the doctor's little figure entered the room.

" Have you finished ? "

" The important business is over, detective, and I'm very much of the opinion that the criminals depended for their safety on the stupidity of a deputy-coroner. They never thought an old gray rat who knows his P's from his Q's would be in the business ! "

" Have you discovered any thing new ? "

" Nothing except the victim is dead ! But while I amuse myself examining a specimen of the blood yonder under a microscope, do you amuse yourself by looking around the room for a stray bullet. You will most probably find it embedded in the wall or woodwork."

The disciplined detective asked no questions, but immediately began his search, while the doctor placed the little microscope he carried in his hand on the desk, drew back the curtain opposite, placed a drop of blood on a glass slide, examined it for a brief moment under the microscope, and then, with hands in pocket, sauntered to one of the bookcases and amused himself by reading the titles on the backs of the books. After a brief interval, he turned and said :

" You have discovered it ? "

" No ; but I will have the room explored inch by inch."

" I am not particular, as I only suggested the search to put your mind in a proper condition to appreciate my discovery. Now, please step here beside me. Here is a pistol which one of your men discovered in the bucket of the well, and which I took from him as he was sneaking along to give it to you!" With the words, he drew a pistol from his pocket and placed it in the detective's hand.

"You will observe, detective, that one of the barrels of the revolver is discharged."

"No doubt of it, doctor!"

"Very well. Now here is the bullet that I extracted from the brain of the dead man. Compare it with the intact bullets in the chambers."

"It is smaller in every way, doctor, and belongs to a different weapon."

"Exactly; and thereby demonstrating that the pistol with which the murder was committed is still to be found."

"The criminal was *not* wise," said the detective, with his eyes resting on the weapon in his hand. "You'll be interested to hear, Captain Travers, that on the handle of this revolver is a silver plate on which are engraved the initials G. D. It's curious how *very* anxious this G. D. is to get himself hung. But tell me, doctor, does your microscope say any thing."

"It has a very strong objection to speak just now. By and by it *may* say something valuable. But I strongly advise you to look for the other pistol."

"If it is to be found, I will find it. In the meantime the captain and I are going on a little exploring expedition."

"Good. I shall remain here till five o'clock; but, I warn you, I will not miss my dinner, even for my friend Travers."

CHAPTER VI.

AN EXPLORING EXPEDITION.

" YOU think the criminal is a woman?" asked the captain, when the detective, after giving a few orders, passed down the veranda steps and was walking briskly toward the village.

" That is my present opinion, and if I am compelled to change it hereafter, I shall feel as if I am not fit for my business."

" Is it not possible that you may be mistaken and hasty?"

" They say that every thing is possible, and I *may* be mistaken, but if every fact we discover does not strengthen my belief, why, my vanity is greater than my prophetic vision. If I could only interview the mysterious G. D., at this moment, a large amount of valuable time might be spared. And yet, if the mysterious *he* is the enemy of the mysterious *she*, we shall be landed in a maze."

" You are speaking as mysteriously as a prophet, detective."

" I am trying to solve the one puzzle that perplexes me. We must either suppose that our G. D. is the most foolish of fools, anxious to throw a noose around his neck, or we must suppose that he

is innocent, and the real guilty party is endeavor-
ing to throw the blame on him. Accepting the latter alternative as the more probable, I boldly assert
that no one but an impulsive, rash woman would
have the audacity to so boldly prepare a trap
for an enemy. She has committed a murder ; but
even the crime has not brought her discretion.
She does not here show ordinary cunning ; she
forces under the eyes of the law what a male criminal, with the same object in view, would force the
law to look for. No one could miss finding the
handkerchief ; nor the pistol. And here is another
point ; she had the pistol in her possession and
discharges one of its chambers, and then uses
another pistol with which to commit the murder !
We have to do with a passionate woman, Captain
Travers, who cares more to accomplish her object
than to plot for her own safety."

"May not both man and woman be guilty ? "

" I have thought of that theory and rejected it.
The initials so boldly displayed are enough to condemn it in my eyes, though, of course, I shall not
neglect it in my investigations. If both *are* concerned, the man is deeply in love or deeply indebted
to the woman. But we need more light on the
antecedents of the dead man. One of the letters
found in his pocket is seemingly from his lawyer, a
Mr. Thomas Terms, whose office is at 40 Myrtle
Avenue, and to Mr. Terms we are now going."

The lawyer's office was easily found ; it was on
the main street of the village. An upright post

upheld a large square of wood bearing, in gigantic
letters, the worthy man's name. Unfortunately,
Mr. Terms was absent, busied with some matters
connected with the murder, and would not return
to the village until late in the evening. A sallow-
faced young man, with faint indications of a red
mustache, gave the information with cheerful
alacrity. This young man was Mr. Abe Clayton,
the lawyer's clerk, and under the skillful questioning of Detective Sharpe he was readily induced to
tell all he knew of the past history of some of the
people involved in the tragedy. In Mr. Clayton's
opinion the object of the murder was robbery. It
seems that, two days before, Mr. Addison had
drawn ten thousand dollars from the bank, or
rather Mr. Terms drew it for him, on one of
his checks. In requesting the lawyer to obtain
the money for him, Mr. Addison explained
that he intended to use it in renovating the old
house. Mr. Clayton expressed the confident
opinion that the murder was committed on account
of this money. Questioned as to whom he suspected as the murderer, Mr. Clayton displayed a
wily reticence, and refused to be "caught". He
insinuated, however, that Mr. Addison was a
"softy" who, when in the village, was always followed by a lot of "beats" intent on borrowing
money, and that it was one of these "beats" who
had committed the murder. On being asked if
he knew any body whose name would fit the initials
G. D., Mr. Clayton winked vigorously, and ex-

pressed the opinion that " Geoffrey Draper was the chap to toe the mark ! " Mr. Clayton believed that Geoffrey Draper had " left the village for the season ". Further questioning drew out the facts that Mr. Draper put on the " airs " of a gentleman, but that he was a fraud. He had once been the friend of the dead man, following him everywhere, but that finally the disgusted Mr. Addison had publicly insulted him, " kicked him down-stairs and given him the dead shake ! " According to Mr. Abe Clayton, Draper accepted the insult and appeared among his friends as quietly as ever. Mr. Clayton concluded his rambling account by branding Geoffrey Draper as " a calf's liver with diluted water instead of blood in his veins. However," he added, forgetting his pride in his officiousness, " if he hasn't left the village, and you'd like to see him, I can give you a lift. Most of his *valuable* correspondence is directed to the care of our P. O. box, and here are a couple of letters for him which you can take up to his house. Its number is 27 on this street, a little distance below here. If he's gone, you can send 'em back."

Detective Sharpe gratefully accepted the mission, and retired from the presence of the young man, after expressing the intention of calling on Mr. Terms.

He had no difficulty in finding Mr. Draper's house, which was an ugly little brick structure, vulgarly pretentious and repelling. The detective, followed by the captain, unhesitatingly walked to the veranda, where a surly-faced servant was lounging on an arm-chair, smoking a pipe. In answer to the question, he condescended to give the information that Mr. Draper was not at home, and that he did not know when he would be at home. " But," he added, with a satirical smile, " you kin wait and try your luck. May be he'll be back next minute, may be next year ! "

He lazily rose, pushed open the front door, and ushered the visitors into a small but tastefully furnished room.

" That's a good portrait," said the smiling detective, pointing to an oil painting that had attracted the attention of Captain Travers the moment he entered the room, and from which he could not withdraw his eyes. It was the " three-quarter " portrait of a handsome man with large russet-colored beard and mustache—the portrait of a face he had seen alive in the moonlight in his lonely watch of last night.

" That's Mr. Draper," said the servant. " If you've got any thing to say you might say it to the pictur' and save time ! "

Detective Sharpe preferred the surly servant as a companion, and he speedily converted him into a very communicative witness, especially when he announced that he was the bearer of a sum of money for his master. The arrival of visitors had attracted a comely woman to the doorway, and the announcement of money stimulated her into saying :

" Then we'll git what's been owed us for the last
three months ; and the grocer and butcher and
baker 'll git paid, too."

The surly man and the comely woman had now
to be restrained in their volubility ; but from
their diffuse statements the following facts were
gained : Mr. Draper was deeply in debt, even to
his servants. On the morning before, the servants
had demanded their money, and Mr. Draper said
that he expected, on that same morning, to receive
the money for a piece of property he had sold,
and that on his return from the city all his debts
would be paid. He had gone out after breakfast
on the day before, and they had not seen him since,
though he had promised to return in a few hours.
Concerning his habits, the cook had much to say ;
a veiled woman or women were coming to the
house at all hours in the day or night, and Mr.
Draper himself opened the door. He had no other
friends in the village but this woman or these
women, " for they may a bin many, for their faces
was always veiled, and all cats is gray in the
dark." Three evenings ago " he had a awful
quarrel with the woman what visited him." Cook,
who was not listening, " heard the woman say,
' You must not risk it ! I love you, and you've
run enough danger for me.' Then I hear a kiss,
and *he* says, ' I'd risk any thing to bring *you*
happiness, my dear.' Then they whisper, and by
and by he says, ' When I get the money we'll start
out on a new plan.' Then she says, ' Any thing

but this life ; it's killing me.'   And then he kisses
and hugs her."

Cook had no idea who the veiled woman was,
but she had rings on her fingers and came in her
carriage.   In cook's opinion, her master had got a
large sum of money, and then run away with it to
escape his creditors, for " he was a wild bad 'un ! "

" A woman came last night ! " said the surly
man.   " I didn't see her face, and I didn't open the
door ; but I looked out the window to tell her
master wasn't home, and I see she was dressed in a
white dress with di'monds flashing in her ears.   If
he'd bin home he'd a let her in."

" Of course he would ! " exclaimed the cook, indignantly.   " Such goings on, and honest helps
can't get their honest earnings.   It's a shame, and
I ain't afraid to say so ! "

The detective had risen and approached a little
round table, on which were several unopened letters.   While speaking his right hand toyed idly
with the envelopes.

" It's hardly worth while waiting here any
longer," he said, with a quick glance at the letters.
" I will come again to-morrow, and I sincerely hope
that Mr. Draper will be at home to receive the
money I bring him ! "

When he left the house one of the letters that
was on the round table reposed snugly in the side
pocket of his coat.

" Your theory is stretching to a dangerously
thin condition, is it not, Detective Sharpe ? "

asked Captain Travers when they had turned their backs on the little brick house.

"It seems so!" was the good-natured answer. "But I still think it is strong enough to hold the guilty party—or parties! If our G. D. is a fool, so much the worse for him. He disappeared at a very unfortunate moment, if he is innocent."

"And if he *is* innocent he did a very foolish thing; for I saw him gazing anxiously up toward the house in which the murdered man's body lay!"

Without further comment Captain Travers described his experience of the night before; that is, the portion that related to the man with the russet whiskers. Through a feeling which he could not account for himself, he still refrained from mentioning the more startling adventure with the mysterious woman.

"So our friend did not run away, after all!" was the detective's criticism. "That is, we can now be certain that he remained in the village till six or seven o'clock last night. That is something gained, something to lean on. According to the testimony of our tramp, a woman was in the house at the same time. Was it a coincidence, or were both working with one object? Did they return for something they had forgotten; or were they seeking for something that they could not find? Was money the only object of the murder, or was it money and something else? Whether he shares the guilt, or is innocent, the solution of the mystery lies with the very foolish G. D!"

" You still hold to the woman theory ? "

"Always," answered the detective with assurance. "She is the heroine and he only a helpless aid, even if he shares the crime. He may have fired the pistol-shot for money, which she clamored for, but *her* object was not money. Her safety depended on the murdered man's silence ; he held some secret that would ruin her. To silence one tool, she used another, and I should not be astonished that to her is due the mysterious disappearance that puzzles us."

" You believe there is another murder ? "

" It would not astonish me ? "

" You have converted a woman into a fiend ! " said the captain with disgust.

" Nature has done so before me ! There is nothing more out-and-out wicked than a conscienceless woman struggling for her own safety. Think over all the facts of the case which we have thus far discovered, and then tell me what you think ; not of my new, but of my reconstructed theory, which, as facts accumulate, I may have to reconstruct and reconstruct again. I make it larger to embrace all the facts ; but from first to last, the nucleus of our snowball remains the same."

" I listen to you with interest and admiration, and if I venture to differ, I use only the privilege you have given me."

" I court your criticism, Captain Travers ! Now listen to the reconstructed hypothesis : Suppose there is a woman moving in the upper circles of

life, respected, honored and admired. Suppose
that, in former days, she has done something
which would degrade her. Suppose that, in some
way, the murdered man was acquainted with the
fact. But he has gone away on a pleasure voyage
without making the fact public. In a little while
news is received that the man and his yacht were
swallowed up in the ocean. Such a fact was
reported in the newspapers of Mr. Addison and *his*
yacht. The woman feels perfectly safe, and
rejoices. Let us suppose, now, that she met with a
man like our G. D. is reported to be, a handsome,
dressy fellow. That he is not her equal, in intellect
or otherwise, makes no difference. Some of your own
aristocratic ladies have run away with coachmen.
We will say that she is smitten with him ; but for
some reason, which I hope to discover, dares not
openly show her infatuation. Perhaps she has parents who know how unworthy G. D. is, and would
sternly forbid any association with him. In any
case she dares not openly marry him ; and neither
possesses enough money to suggest an elopement.
While the annoyances naturally incident to such a
state of affairs are accumulating, the supposed
dead man returns to life. He threatens the woman;
—if he loves her he will surely do so ! At least we
will, temporarily, suppose that his reappearance
places her in a dangerous position. On a certain
day he withdraws ten thousand dollars from the
bank for his own use. The woman hears of this and
uses it as a means of stimulating G. D. to robbery

and murder. The fool falls into the trap, and when he has served the purpose of doing what she alone could not do, she quietly gets rid of him ; in what way I am not yet prepared to say. When she has made him vanish, she has so arranged it that suspicion shall all point to him, even his disappearance adding a finishing touch to the clumsy but not inartistic work ! If you ask me why she visited the house after the crime, I will answer that it was in connection with the secret. She tore the leaves out of the memorandum-book, and did other things which I will discover when I go carefully over the house this evening. At least that is my rough theory which I give you in accordance with the promise that you should see and hear all I do and think in the working up of this case. Ponder it in bed to-night, and the weakness that you discover I may be able to strengthen when we meet again tomorrow."

They had reached the old house by this time. Dr. Dubois was pacing slowly up and down the veranda, enjoyingly puffing at a cigar ; and with hands clasped behind his back. He had plucked a small bouquet of choice flowers, and thrust them in the lapel button-hole of his black frock-coat, and every now and then he bent his head and inhaled their perfume. He greeted his friend with a pleasant smile, and glanced at the detective with an amused expression on his face, and in his bright gray eyes.

"Is the coroner within, doctor ?"

" No ; he has gone to the city. The inquest is adjourned for a week ! "

" Was nothing done ? "

" Yes, a jury empaneled, and the dead body looked at."

" No evidence taken at all ? "

" None ! "

" That is remarkably stupid even for a coroner."

" Judgments are as various as tastes," said the doctor gayly, " and talking of tastes suggests that it is almost time to go home to dinner. It's five o'clock, Travers, and if you are going back with me it s time to move ! I suppose, detective, you remain all night here ? "

" I shall not sleep until I have thoroughly examined the house."

" Well, you won't die of loneliness or of lack of stimulation to work." He turned to a tall, gray-haired man, who at the moment came out on the veranda, and said, " Max, this is Detective Sharpe, who has staked his reputation on bringing your master's murderer to justice. Detective, this is Max Newton, who has sworn to devote his life to revenging his master's murder ! "

CHAPTER VII.

WISDOM AND BEAUTY.

" I AM not sorry to escape to more congenial company," said the doctor, thrusting his arm through that of his friend. " Sharpe is just a trifle of a bore ! "

" I hope Miss Gower is better ! " said the captain, somewhat irrelevantly, yet unable longer to suppress the anxiety that had haunted him all day.

" Keep your common-sense, Travers. She is probably out of her narcotized state, and will look very interesting with her pale face and elaborate dress. But don't make a fool of yourself. Listen to the birds, and *think* your romance."

" I will not trouble you now ; but I must have your advice ! "

" Keep it till I come into your room to-night. I am in a mood to dream of the luxuries that the little treasure, Percy, has prepared for my special delight. I surrender the nightingale to you ; leave me, then, to the memory of chicken croquettes."

The homeward journey was made in silence, both men becoming absorbed in their thoughts. No news waited for them at their journey's end. Miss Gower had remained all day in her room, but, according to her maid, was more comfortable, though still under the influence of the drug.

The doctor heartily enjoyed the excellent dinner, but Captain Travers sat at the table merely out of ceremony, every moment seeming an hour, and every word irritating his sense of hearing like loud peals from a funeral bell. The doctor and his host spoke of the condition of Miss Gower ; Mr. Morris uttered the belief that she was a confirmed opium-eater and expressed the intention of placing her in an asylum for the cure of the disease, to which the doctor nodded vigorous assent.

Captain Travers retired to his room at the first opportunity, and passed several very weary hours in restlessly pacing up and down. The rustling of a dress in the hall seemed to stimulate him to a certain resolution. He approached the door, and as Miss Percy passed by it, on her way to the hall, he said :

" Pardon me ; but I found this little thing near the house to-day. Perhaps it belongs to you."

With the words he withdrew a small shawl from his pocket and placed it in her hands.

" It belongs to Miss Gower," said the maid, positively, " and disappeared mysteriously yesterday. With your permission I will take possession of it in my mistress's name."

" Of course," laughed the captain, nervously. " If it is hers ! "

" It *is* hers, and there is not another like it in the country."

" Then keep it, by all means. Can you kindly inform me where the doctor is ? "

" He expressed the determination to write out his report before he retired. Do you wish to see him ? "

" No ! no ! " groaned the captain. " If I could forget myself I would be happy."

The doctor was in the library, where every thing had been arranged for his comfort. On a little side-table near the desk were cigars, a plate of dainty biscuits, and a bottle of his favorite wine.

" She is a treasure ! Her unconventional simplicity is charming ! She deserves a better fate than destiny metes out to her ! " The worthy doctor yawned ; the wine he had drunk at dinner made him sleepy, and he was not in a mood for the serious work before him. But, scorning ease when duty claimed him, he seated himself at the desk, and soon became absorbed in his work, his pen racing furiously over the paper, scrawling hiero-glyphics rather than words.

He was in the midst of an intricate subject, when there was a discreet tap on the door, and in answer to his permission, Miss Percy entered the room. She had doffed her formal attire, and her slender figure was draped in a loose robe. Her hair had also been released from the restraint of its classical Greek band, and fell in uncontrolled freedom over neck and bosom, a simple blue ribbon partially restraining its rippling wantonness.

" I came to see if you needed any thing before I retired," she said, standing near the doorway.

"You have anticipated all my wants, Miss Percy, and I shall feel reproached if you dim your pretty eyes by keeping awake on my account."

"I never sleep more than four hours; I have learned French and Italian in the time that I have stolen from sleep; and when I was a child I always studied my lessons in bed—that is, after my maid was asleep. All my energies are most active in the night."

"I wish mine were at the present moment. I am compelled to send a long business document away early in the morning, and in my eagerness I write so illegibly that I shall be compelled to correct my spots of ink into readable English."

"Would you allow me to play the part of amanuensis?" asked the young woman, timidly. "I do not write badly for a woman, and it would be a great happiness to assist you, even as a copyist."

"You could not read a word of my scrawl," said the doctor, eying the manuscript before him.

"May I make the attempt?"

He handed her a sheet of paper with a smile, and to his astonishment she read it with unhesitating facility.

"Listen, please: 'You must be particular in every detail. I shall feel disappointed if we do not demonstrate my theory of the case without the chance of an objection. It will not be the first time that science has vindicated justice, and reproved blundering self-assurance. Murder is bad enough!'" Miss Percy looked up from the page with a smile of triumph.

"You read without hesitation where I myself would have stumbled!" said the doctor, with unconcealed admiration.

"Before you decide you must see my hand-writing."

She leaned over the desk so close to him that a stray lock of her perfumed hair fell on his shoulder, and wrote, with a bold, free hand :

> "'You say, not always wisely, know thyself !
> Know others, ofttimes is the better maxim.'

"To Professor Dubois from his ignorant, yet devoted friend,   MAY PERCY."

"You write superbly, and are very heroic in your desire to help, but the subject is hardly fitted for you to read."

With a glance of gay defiance, she seized the pages of manuscript from the table and read them to the end. "There is nothing here, sir, that a school-girl dare not read."

"I had not reached the real subject, when you appeared. But you have given me the excuse for idleness."

"I am sorry for disturbing you, and for reading your manuscript, for it recalls my father's death, and though the doctors said otherwise, I still believe he was poisoned by his cruel second wife. I have been told—am I wrong?—that there are some agents that may destroy life without leaving any traces behind?"

" In the present state of science that is almost an impossibility. Science is not infallible," said the doctor, admiring the graceful pose of his young friend, and the child-like interest revealed in her pretty face, " but *I* have never seen the poison that I could not discover. I know a case "—the doctor suddenly paused, then said with dry dogmatism : " No, I have never been deceived ! I have made mistakes," he added, speedily recovering his good humor, " but I have found them out before they caused any trouble. Criminals, even when most clever and attractive, do some little thing or leave something undone, which reveals the cloven hoof. Take the case of Mr. Addison, for example ! "

In her interest in the conversation she had placed her little clasped hands on the doctor's knee, and there was an expression of absorbed attention in her face. In a fatherly way, he gently patted her on the head.

" This horrible talk will give you the nightmare, my child."

" I am very much interested. You were saying ? "

" You have very pretty hair. If I were younger——"

" Please do not descend to common flattery," she pleaded, somewhat impatiently. " Interest me with your conversation," she said, with a fine smile, " and I shall not remember the boldness of your hand. You were speaking of the stupidity of criminals,"

" I was taking the case of Mr. Addison as an example of it," he said, toying with a strand of her hair.
" The criminal shoots his victim in the skull and
then leaves his pistol to reveal his crime. Here
you find *I* will not hesitate. You shall copy my
report of the case to-morrow, and you will see that
I boldly stake my reputation on the pistol bullet
being the cause of death."

Miss Percy sighed, as if a weight were lifted
from her mind, then smiled gayly, glancing sideways
at his bold hand.

" I am tired of seriousness, and my recollection
of the proprieties is coming back. As you are so
very good, I will weave you a watch-chain out of
the hair your wisdom so much admires."

" I will wear it all my life, and it shall be buried
with me ! "

She glanced at him with doubtful, then with
pleased surprise, and a subtile smile curled her
ripe lips.

" You teach me I am still human ! " she said
softly. He had risen, and she now rose and stood
beside him.

" You regret your promise ? "

" It has not been sealed."

With a gay smile, not without its element of sad-
ness, he pressed his lips to her soft cheeks. She
started back with a flush and frown which speedily
dissolved into a troubled smile.

" We know each other now ! " she said, in a
forced voice. " Farewell till to-morrow ! "

With a mocking courtesy and a light laugh, she turned and quitted the room.

" Little Judas ! She is young to indulge in that kind of treachery. But she is an expert and very attractive, even though her soft hair become a noose that will choke her ! "

CHAPTER VIII.

ON this same night Detective Sharpe is weaving a noose in which hemp takes the place of hair. The evening is still young, and he is sitting in the library with the venerable servant, Max, as a companion. He has discovered that the old man's frank face is a true index of his heart ; and Detective Sharpe is noted for his thorough knowledge of human nature.

With praiseworthy self-repression, Max Newton does not allow his personal feelings to lead him into exaggeration or morbid sentiment. He answers the questions addressed to him with grave unhesitancy, yet with a calm deliberation, as if his reverence of truth were even greater than his agony at the death of a beloved master. He carefully distinguishes between suspicions and facts, and has deliberately delivered the statement, that he would rather prefer the guilty wretch should escape than that his soul should be blackened by even the shadow of a false charge. A solitary candle is burning on the desk, and casts a dim light on his pale and seriously sorrowful face.

Lying before the detective is the crimson-bound

memorandum book which he had abstracted from the bookcase earlier in the day, and the conversation revolves around it as a center.

According to Mr. Newton, his master had no vices. Mr. Addison was "a large-hearted noble gentleman". As a child he was sad and self-repressed, and inherited some of the eccentricities of his grandfather " who was haunted with the idea that his enemies were bent on murdering him". Under this fear he built *Lesbia* Villa, planning " hiding-places in case of surprise, and with mysterious doors of exit for the purposes of escape". The boy Hugo loved solitude and developed such strange fancies that his parents became alarmed, and finally determined that he must have a companion who, when he grew to man's estate, was to become his wife. They wrote to one of their distant friends who was poor and burdened with a large family ; and a wearisome correspondence ended by the friends sending one of their daughters to the house. The boy became the slave of the girl, and her presence produced the effects that the fond parents had hoped for. A number of tranquil, happy years passed by, but as the girl advanced to womanhood she became, in Mr. Newton's language, a " thoughtless, heartless coquette ". Fortunately, her adopted parents did not live to witness her complete transformation.

" They died," said Mr. Newton, solemnly, " in ignorance of the storm that was gathering over the head of their beloved son, and he inherited their

wealth. The girl, who had been a flirt, now became
a prude, and refused to live under the same roof
with her intended husband."

The patient Mr. Addison secured for her a
little cottage which " he furnished with elegance ".
The girl and her maid removed to her new quarters
after the funeral of her adopted parents, and Mr.
Addison, having " a horror of the house in which his
parents died ", leased another little cottage for
himself at the other end of the village. The girl,
according to Mr. Newton, now threw aside all
restraint. Mr. Geoffrey Draper had come to the
village, and he became her especial favorite. Mr.
Addison angrily expostulated with her, but she
defied him. In Max Newton's language, " she had
developed into a fiend ". In her malice she wrote
letter after letter to Mr. Addison, charging him with
all kinds of cruelties and absurdities. She refused
to see him ; she refused to marry him. Mr.
Addison was plunged into the deepest grief by
these actions.

" His heart was broken," said Mr. Newton, with
the tears welling up to his eyes. " He tried to
escape from his troubles ; he speculated in stocks,
he bought a yacht, and he sailed for a year anywhere, everywhere, and I believe he is happier now
than when he was alive. As to the woman, she
left the house he had provided for her and went
elsewhere, and for a year, as I am informed, has
been living to please herself." ·

" Where are the letters she wrote to him ? "

" I do not know. But, surely, somewhere in this house."

" You can give me no other information on this point ? "

The old man hesitated ; a spasm passed over his face, and his eyes filled with tears.

" Mine is a sad position, Detective Sharpe ! " he said in a trembling voice. " To revenge my dear master's death I would willingly lay down my own life ; but in avenging it I am compelled to act contrary to my master's orders. Time and time again he has said to me, ' Spare her, Max, at whatever cost ! If she outlives me, and I have a presentiment she will, she must live honored and respected by the world.' If I ever dared to speak harshly of her—I held him in my arms when he was a child, and he tolerated me !—he would place his hands over my lips and, with a sad smile, repeat : ' Spare her now and always ! I love her, Max ! The ideal is grown into my life, and the reality has no power to destroy it. She will repent one day ! ' "

" I appreciate your loyal affection to a kind master ; but, at the same time, you have a duty to perform to the world and to morality. I hope you do not wish the criminal to escape."

" Not if it were my own *sister !* " said the old man, impetuously.

The detective felt a pleasant glow of satisfaction, and secretly congratulated himself on his own cunning and his companion's simplicity.

"Let us now return to the letters, Mr. Newton, and please tell me all you know."

The old man took a crumpled piece of paper from his pocket and said :

"A few days after our return here from a year's absence, I received orders to take the yacht down to the city to have it cleaned. Before surrendering it at the ship-yard, I looked around to see that nothing of value had been left aboard. In the waste-basket in my master's cabin I discovered this unfinished draught of a letter."

The detective hastily seized the paper and read :

"MY LIFE AND LOVE :

"Your letter reached me after my long absence, but its cruelty had no power to prevent the thrill of delight its receipt gave me. I can not, I dare not, accede to your request, which would rob me of my vindication in the eyes of the world. But more—I still love you, even if you hate me in return, and in my love I must have some hold over you. You are free to do all you wish, and with my life and my fortune I will assist you to what *you* believe is your future happiness, *I*, your misery. You have been reckless, cruel and unjust ; but I forgive you, and love you, or rather, the ideal which has been knitted into my very soul. But I must keep those letters, not for the world's eyes, but for my own happiness. They have blasted my life, but they are part of my past. To part with them would be to part with my soul. No eyes but my own will ever see them. Even should your words come true and I meet an unexpected death—I wish, with you, that the report of my disaster had proved true!—they are so safely concealed in the secret drawer of my dear mother's cabinet that they will never be found. Threats are useless ; I do not love life enough to fear them. You have ruined it ; but I will not reproach you. What my love can not surrender, your covert threats can not wrest from me. I may die suddenly—"

The fragment abruptly ended with these ominous words.

"This is very suggestive, Mr. Newton, and very valuable. Do you know where the cabinet is to which it refers?"

"Yes," said the old man, sadly.

"We will pay it a visit; but first let me clearly understand a few points. As I understand it, the woman's conduct was so shameless after the death of the people who had adopted her, that your master refused to marry her."

"She refused to marry him ; refused his repeated offers ; and he finally tacitly accepted the inevitable as the best. I fear he was so much infatuated that had she, at any time, wished to entrap him into wedlock, he would have yielded even with his eyes opened, as they were. Fearing this, and to escape from her and himself, he forced himself to undergo a year's aimless wanderings in his yacht."

"Was he paying for her support all this time?"

"She owed every thing to him till she left the

house he had provided for her, and then he was compelled to withdraw his support."

" Did she ever visit Mr. Geoffrey Draper at his house on Myrtle Avenue ? "

" Personally, I know nothing ; but I have heard —you can easily find people who will verify the statement—I have heard that she frequently visited the man, and that letters, which she was particularly anxious to receive secretly, were directed to her in the care of Mr. Draper."

" She was evidently very fond of him."

" It may have been love, or something else. At least, he was very attentive to her and she to him."

" Do you know any thing of his antecedents ? "

" I only know him as he appeared here. He was introduced to my master by a common friend, and he was received as a friend until he revealed his true nature. He is without conscience ; and yet, if he was the best of men, what can be said of a young woman who, alone, entered his house at night, as report said she did ? A vulgar gambler ! "

" Ten thousand dollars would be a temptation there, surely ! " said the detective musingly. " You tell me that when you went down to the city, on the evening preceding the day of the murder, he had the money ? "

" I saw him lock it in the drawer of the desk in the library ; and, at my request, he slept in this house over night to guard it, instead of going elsewhere. It was to have been personally carried by me, on my return next day, to the people for whom it was drawn."

"And not a cent of it can be discovered !" said the detective, staring at the pictures opposite. "He was *not* her enemy, and, as I thought, she had taken advantage of his blind trust in her. Did the woman know he was staying at the house ? "

"She knew he was in the village, and he had written to her that he would meet her at the lawyer's office on the next day ; that is, the day of his death. But Mr. Terms, the lawyer, can give you more information on this point than I can. He was one of my master's trusted friends."

"What became of the maid that waited on the woman ? "

"Her mistress unceremoniously discharged her when she left the cottage ; and, as she had no friends in the country, my master paid her passage back over the ocean, that she might return to her relatives. He was thoughtful and noble in every thing."

The detective consulted his note-book, then asked :

"Do you know any thing of a young woman called May Percy ? "

"Nothing, sir ! "

"Have you ever heard of the name ? "

"I have heard that a very excellent young woman of that name lived in the village ; but I never saw her. Mr. Terms has lived here all his life, and he can give you information on that point, as well as on every thing else connected with local history."

"Will you show me now where the cabinet is ?"

"It is in a bed-room that has not been opened since its angel occupant died. The door was kept locked, and my master trusted no one but himself with the key. I fear we shall not be able to get in."

"Show me the room and I will have the door forced open to-morrow."

The old man seized the light, and, followed by the detective, passed along a dreary hall that dismally echoed back their footsteps. They then descended a broad flight of stairs.

"The room is at the end of this passage-way. The door is too heavy for us to force without tools."

"Let me see it, at least."

They paused before a massive oak-door hidden in a gloomy angle.

"We shall require no key, Mr. Newton," said the detective, with an oath. "Some one has been here before us, and forced an entrance into the room. See! the lock is broken, and the door yields to the slightest push !"

"I am dazed, sir !"

"We have been anticipated, and I fear our best card is stolen from us. You must reserve your dismay and surprise for another occasion. Please show me the way."

They entered a huge room whose atmosphere chilled the blood. Nothing was visible in the dim

light but the salient points of pieces of furniture.
The detective stumbled against a chair, which was
massive enough to bear the contact without moving an inch from its place.

"The cabinet is in yonder corner, detective,
between the two windows."

It was a large cabinet, built of heavy, black
wood and richly carved with figures and flowers;
a solid, artistic, serviceable piece of work, the
art of making which our century seems to
have lost. Unfortunately, a vandal hand had
marred its beauty; a panel had been brutally
smashed in one of the doors, and an ax,
or some other sharp instrument, had chopped
away the floor of the little closet on which it
opened.

"Was the secret drawer beneath this closet, Mr.
Newton?"

"Yes, sir!"

"Then I was right," said the detective, after
passing his hand into the cavity beneath. "The
letters have been stolen!"

"But it was a secret drawer only known to my
master," retorted the old man, with superstitious
horror.

"Your memory is weak. Is it not possible that
his adopted sister should know as much of this
cabinet as the little boy? She must have seen it a
great many times."

"You are right," said the old man, in a whisper.
"As children, both have played with the figures on

the cabinet and hidden their toys in the secret drawer ! "

" The same hand that tore the tell-tale leaves from the memorandum-book stole the letters ; and its owner was thoroughly acquainted with the house and the habits of its master. The robbery is more convincing than the letters would have been. Please hand me the candle a moment, Mr. Newton."

He passed the light into the little closet and studied the wood-work with deep interest.

" There is blood on this projecting piece of jagged wood ! " he exclaimed, with smiling satisfaction. " The thief, in her haste to reach the letters, has scraped her hand or arm against the sharp point. She has given us some evidence in return for what she has stolen, and I shall make full use of it. We have no further business in this room to-night, Mr. Newton. Let us return to the library."

Once more sitting before the desk in the room where the crime was committed, the detective studied the candle-flame for some time in silence, his thoughts busied piecing together the fragments of evidence he had gathered. The servant sat on the lounge a short distance away, outside the dim circle of light.

" The robbery is a bad stroke of luck for me, Mr. Newton," said the detective, suddenly breaking the silence. " Out of those letters I should have been able to weave the rope that would hang your master's murderer. We do not even know the nature of their contents."

"The wretch has been bolder than I believed possible," sighed the old man, in turn rousing himself from his reverie ; "and all scruples have vanished. I read those letters, Detective Sharpe, unknown to my master, but in his interest."

"I am not a moralist," said the detective, eagerly, "and I am so grateful to your curiosity that I forgive your former reticence. What was their nature ? "

"They degraded the hand that wrote them. Openly confessed her shame."

"The woman had fallen ? "

"Yes ; the first letter was a confession of her degradation, and plea for assistance. The woman humbled herself in repentance when repentance was too late to save her honor. I know my master did not write any answers to these letters, and when I read them I understood the agony, shame and grief into which they had thrown him. Receiving no answer, the woman wrote again, and again ; her cries for mercy gradually changed into threats that, unless her demands for money and other assistance were complied with, she would accuse her noble, innocent protector of being the cause of her ruin, and publicly disgrace him. Fortunately, the first letter completely disproved the last, and I suppose this is one reason why my master refused to surrender them. Any other man than Mr. Addison would have allowed the vile woman to rot in her degradation ; he did nothing more cruel than to send her money anonymously. She went to the city for a short time, and when she returned she was all meekness and self-reproach. She wrote a number of letters asking for pardon and mercy, and, at the time, my master was so touched by them, that I was compelled to use force to prevent him rushing to her with the guilty letters, for the return of which she earnestly pleaded. He yielded to my arguments, and it is now my greatest sorrow that I ever uttered them."

" You have a theory at last, Mr. Newton ? " said the detective, with a triumphant smile.

" He was dealing with a fiend ! " answered the old man excitedly, and nervously clutching at his white hair. " She was winning her way into respectability again, and her past was a menace to her. She needed the letters, and a murder was committed that she might obtain them. Curse her ! "

The sudden change to wild passion astonished the detective, and he dismissed the heartbroken servant for the night.

" Poor devil, it has used him up ! " he reflected as he stretched himself on the lounge. " That breed of servants has long since died out."

He suddenly remembered that he had in his pocket three letters—two given him by Mr. Terms's clerk and one which he had purloined from Mr. Draper's house. He had determined to read them, but he was drowsy, and deferred this piece of illegality to a more favorable opportunity. He sank

into a condition which was neither sleep nor wake-
fulness ; consciousness remained, while his body lost
its power of moving. At the same time he seemed
to hear the pattering of light footsteps and the
rustling of a woman's dress. Was he dreaming ?
A strange, yet familiar odor now assailed his
nostrils ; yet before it had completely conquered his
senses, he saw through his drooping eyelids the
outline of a human form. The face was above and
outside the line of vision, and he had not the power
to adjust himself so as to catch a glimpse of it ; but
he saw the attire ; a creamy mull, ornamented with
knots of pale-blue ribbon ; he felt a warm breath on
his forehead, and hands busied with the pockets of
his coat—and then he sank into unconsciousness.

CHAPTER IX.

A LEGAL OPINION.

WHEN Detective Sharpe opened his eyes in the morning, he felt unaccountably drowsy, and when he rose from the lounge his legs were strangely weak in the joints. He stared about him in a vague, perplexed manner ; then, remembering his vision, hastily thrust his hand in the breast pocket of his coat. The mutilated memorandum-book and the three unopened letters which it held had disappeared. Continuing his search, he discovered that his own note-book, in which he had jotted down his ideas, suspicions and intentions concerning the murder, had also vanished ! His humiliation was greater than his anger ; he, the great Detective Sharpe, had been openly robbed by the very people whom he was hunting down. They had boldly defied him, boldly chloroformed him, and plunged their blood-stained hands into his pockets. Yes ! and the tell-tale blue ribbon, which he had found on the hook behind the curtain, had also been stolen ! He turned his pockets inside out, and the fact was undoubted.

"You shall swing for it just the same, my dear," he murmured, with a vicious grinding of the teeth.

" Detective Sharpe is not to be despised with impunity !"

Performing a hasty toilet, for the hour was late, he gave some orders to his assistants and then left the house, and in the open air came face to face with Dr. Dubois.

" Where are you going, Sharpe ? "

" To pay a visit to Mr. Terms."

" I'll go with you, in place of Captain Travers, whose experiences of yesterday have sickened him of the entire business. But you are looking pale, Sharpe."

" I'm feeling in excellent health, and I know I'm in excellent spirits."

" Every thing going on all right ? "

" Yes, and I'm in hopes of speedily bringing the business to a happy conclusion. I mean happy for me."

" It will add immeasurably to your brilliant reputation, " said the doctor, seriously as to face, yet with a secret enjoyment of his own wit.

" I will do my best," answered the detective, with much humility. " But I hope the illustrious Mr. Terms is at home this time."

Mr. Terms was in his office, and he cordially welcomed his guests; but with a certain distinction. He bowed respectfully when the great doctor's name was mentioned, but greeted the detective with a dignified nod of the head, only accepting him as an object whom he could use as lay figure—to talk to, poke at with a long, bony finger, and otherwise

for his own exaltation. He leaned back in his
chair, raised his spectacles from his eyes to his
forehead, placed the fingers of his hands together
over his shrunken abdomen, slowly twirled his
thumbs around, and, in answer to a question, rushed
at once into conversation that threatened to be a
monologue.

"Did I know the lamented deceased? Who
knew him better? who longer? who more inti-
mately? I was at one and the same time his
legal adviser and his friend. For twenty
long years I have known him, shared his
joys and sorrows, and guided his youthful
inexperience with such stores of wisdom as I
possess!"

"And his disposition?"

"Plastic, sir, and amiable. Ready to profit by
advice and to respond to the words of affection."

"Gay?"

"Gay, sir; but only in a moral sense," said Mr.
Terms, with dignified asperity. "He was young,
sir, without the sins of youth; human clay, if you
wish it, but spotless even under the microscope."

"Then his love for his adopted sister——"

"Was his first and only love, sir. All his affection centered in her, and when she left him she
took all his affection with her. He was rich, and
many young women aimed the shafts of love at
him; but, if you will pardon the metaphor, they

never hit the bull's eye. He loved once, and never loved again."

"Are you acquainted with the cause which drove the lady from him ?"

"I *am*, sir, " answered Mr. Terms, severely ; "and it is not to her credit. You shall hear, Detective Sharpe, and you shall judge ! She was taken from very poor people when she was a mere child, and became more than a daughter to our dead friend's parents. She received the best education and the best care. She was thus cultivated and thus reared with the especial understanding that, ultimately, she was to become the wife of our dead client. But, sir, when she had budded into womanhood, and her adopted mother had been added to the silent majority, and she presided at the head of the table as the only surviving specimen of womanhood, she developed traits that had hitherto been latent. She always had a violent temper, flying into spasms of rage for any reason or no reason at all ; but now, sir, she grew obstinate, spiteful, self-willed, vindictive. In place of preserving the sweet isolation in which she was brought up, she insisted on mingling with the giddy throng ; she insisted on flirting and, as *I* think, helped to drive her adopted father to his grave. Until two years ago she seemed to have a certain respect for the proprieties ; but then, sir, she threw off all restraint, and this, sir, in the very cottage our revered martyr provided for her. She refused to see him, and, sir," said Mr. Terms, meaningly, and with terrible emphasis, "she saw others; and the others was a man!"

"I am carried away by the vivid style of your narrative," said the detective; "but before I forget, you will allow me to ask a few questions?"

"I am at your service, Detective Sharpe."

"When the woman's adopted parents were alive I presume she acted with propriety?"

"Not in the way I would have *my* daughter act; but at that time, if she were guilty of indiscretions the world was not allowed to see them."

"According to the best of your knowledge, she was content with the conditions imposed on her?"

"She was cunning, sir; for it was an especial clause in the will of her adopted father that, unless she married his son, she was to go out into the world with only enough money to supply her absolute necessities."

"You saw the will?"

"I held it in my possession four long years, and I opened it. The son inherited all; the woman nothing!"

"While the parents were alive what was the relation of the two young people to each other?"

"*He* was all warmth and affection; *she* all coldness. I have seen him place his arm around her waist and kiss her, and I have seen her struggle against this very natural affection with signs of horror and disgust in her face. Once, sir, I unwittingly entered a room wherein the young couple were, and I heard her threaten to kill herself if he continued to honor her with his love ! The word *honor*, sir, is mine, not hers. No, sir, she never loved him ; she wanted to be a rich man's wife, that was all ! "

" Now, Mr. Terms, discarding all gossip, I would ask you what you personally *know* of the woman's conduct after she left the house of her adopted parents ? "

" Well, sir, I *know* that a man named Geoffrey Draper visited her at all hours, and I *know* that she visited Geoffrey Draper at all hours. It was vile, unpardonable, wicked!" said Mr. Terms, indignantly.

" Who is this Mr. Draper ? "

" A nonentity who appeared here some years ago —I *think* it was the same year in which our hero's parents died. Where he came from, except the slums of the great city, I don't know ; but, for a time, he was very intimate with our distinguished martyr. He is a plausible, well-dressed fellow, and has hired a house here ; but all the money he owns he earned at the gaming table or borrowed from his friends ! "

" Are there gambling houses here, Mr. Terms ? " asked the doctor, speaking for the first time.

" No, sir ! " answered Mr. Terms proudly. " Cypressville is above such immorality ! "

" Then," continued the doctor, "this man Draper did *not* indulge in his evil propensities here ? "

" No, sir ; he played an evil game in a city of evils."

" Then," persisted the doctor, "you have no personal knowledge that this man Draper was a gambler?"

"It is not likely!" said Mr. Terms, somewhat disconcerted. "But every body knows he *is* a gambler, and *I* know that his being a gambler is one of the causes which led to a rupture between him and my murdered friend ; for this fact I had from Mr. Addison's own lips!"

"It is very strong evidence," answered the doctor. "Forgive my questions."

"They honor me!"

"Once more, Mr. Terms," said the detective. "Was the final rupture due to the woman or the man now dead?"

"You shall hear, gentlemen, and what I now repeat I had from the lips of Mr. Addison himself, and he was above exaggeration, as he was above all other faults! In this very room he told me of the shameful actions of the woman with strange men."

"With strange men, or a strange man?" again asked the doctor.

"I see I must be rigidly scientific in my language in presence of a scientist," said Mr. Terms. "To be accurate, then, Mr. Addison, with tears in his eyes, complained of the woman's conduct with this Geoffrey Draper. He told me he had spoken to her and she had boldly defied him. Later, after she had closed her door against him, he came to me asking my advice. The woman, sir, had the audacity to charge him with being the cause of what resulted from her own shameless conduct ;

in other words she was using her own disgrace to levy black-mail against an innocent man. On my advice he kept all the letters, while refusing to answer any."

" Did you see these letters, Mr. Terms ? "

" No, but my friend told me of their contents ; and if immorality and black-mail were hanging matters, the letters would have supplied the rope."

" Did Mr. Addison ever make a will ? "

" You are coming to the vital point ! Some years ago he did make a will, which I drew up for him. That will is now in my possession, unopened, as when he delivered it to me."

" What was its nature ? "

" He left every thing he possessed, and without a restricting clause, to the woman whom he expected to become his wife."

" Did he never alter it ? "

" I am coming to that, sir, and I beg all your attention. Time and time again I begged him, in the cause of justice and morality, to alter the will ; but with a sad smile he always put it off, saying, that if he should die his kindness would be the woman's greatest punishment. He was infatuated with her to the end ! Before he went away on his long yacht-voyage, I again argued with him, and he laughingly said he would discuss the subject when he returned. I indignantly urged : 'But if you die, sir, the heartless woman will inherit every thing, and go on her way rejoicing.' 'It will be a test of heaven's desire,' he answered. 'If I die,

I am satisfied that it is heaven's intention to save her in that way. If I live, I will take it as a sign that heaven wishes to punish her, and I will alter the will ! ' "

" He was a crank, like his grandfather ! " was the detective's irreverent comment.

" He was weak when he should have been strong. But let me finish. He returned, and two days before he was murdered he came to me, and I drew up a new will at his request, in which he gave to his 'adopted sister ', as he called her, only enough money to bring her in a modest income ; the rest was given to a number of worthy charities. This new will was to have been signed and sealed on the very day he was murdered ! "

" Of course the woman was not acquainted with this new phase in her destiny ? "

"Yes, sir, she was !" said Mr. Terms, impressively. " He was too honorable to keep her in ignorance. As she was aware of the provisions of the first will, he deemed it his duty to notify her of the change in his intentions, or rather, to be accurate, he deputed me to write to her. Here is a copy of my letter."

Without pausing in his speech, Mr. Terms had opened a book, and was ready at the proper time to read the following letter:

" MADAM :

" I am requested by my client, Mr. Hugo Addison, to notify you, that it is his intention to modify his will. He sacrifices his own feelings to what he conceives to be his duty. He intends to sign this new will on the morning of the 13th September, and he would be pleased to see you or your deputy on, or before, the morning of the said day at the office of the undersigned, that no injustice may be done."

"That was the letter, but the new will was never signed, for foul murder swept him into the grave, and the woman still inherits all his wealth and possessions. The value will be enormous, too, for he speculated lavishly."

"This woman is Miss Gower, the niece of your friend Morris," said the detective, gravely, to the doctor.

"I hope, detective, that you appreciate the value of my communication," added Mr. Terms, impressively, "and if I have been the means of helping justice and morality, gentlemen, I shall feel more than repaid!"

"He is an impressive piece of parchment!" said the doctor, when they had emerged into the open air. "I suppose you mean to arrest Miss Gower, now?"

"What else *can* I do?"

"You have reached your conclusion quicker than I have. But, if you please, let me ask you a question, Sharpe. Of what do you suppose the lamented hero died!"

"Of a pistol-bullet in the brain!"

"As our friend Parchment would say, if a false

conclusion were a crime, you would be hung, Sharpe. Your supposition is entirely wrong ! Let me inform you the bullet was fired in the man's brain *after* he was dead ! "

" Are you sure ? " asked the detective, with unconcealed surprise.

" You forget who is delivering a judgment now ! "

" Pardon me ; but the announcement is so unexpected that it dazes me ! "

" It is nevertheless true, and what is more, Sharpe, is, that the blood which was under the dead man's head was not human blood ! The parties who committed the crime were very anxious to have it believed that he died from a pistol-shot—why, I don't pretend to know !—but they bungled their work outrageously."

" Of what then *did* the victim die."

" I can not answer, and that is why I have not mentioned the subject to you before, although I took the coroner into my confidence. I believe he was poisoned, and acting under this belief I have sent portions of the body to the city to have them properly analyzed."

" What poison do you suspect ? "

" I can not say, as I am not acquainted with the symptoms in life, and there are no characteristic symptoms after death. Probably a narcotic, from the absence of inflammation or erosions. But a poison of some kind surely. If Miss Gower is guilty, she must have forced the poison down her victim's throat, and then killed a number of chickens and used their blood, *after* shooting her victim in the head, *after* he died of poison. She wanted to make sure that she would be found out!"

" But the same objections may be urged by the murderer, whoever he or she may be."

" You are not clear-witted this morning, Sharpe. Go back a few steps; recall the blood on the ivy, the blood on the handkerchief, and, especially, the pistol with the initials on it, and the chamber discharged of a bullet, which was *not* the bullet discovered in the dead man's brain. What is the conclusion of common sense?"

" What I have always maintained; that is, that the guilty party is trying to force the crime on another, with whom she was once intimate."

" That is clumsy. Suppose, now, that there was a third party, who knowing the past history of the dead man and living woman thoroughly, committed the crime. Suppose, also, that our G. D. was deliberately seized on as a pointer to fasten the crime on a woman who was innocent of it. Suppose the third party argued somewhat in this way: ' I will throw G. D's. blood-stained handkerchief in the ivy; his pistol in the well. The clever detectives will discover these objects, and they will immediately know that a man committing a crime will not leave such evidence behind him. The detectives will say, some one is trying to fasten the crime on an innocent man, and they will infallibly be guided to the woman. She will receive all the attention, while I dance in security in the background. She is innocent ; but her past history, related by the exaggerated tongue of scandal, will condemn her past all hope of saving ! ' It is not my business to find out who this third party is. I only wish to show you that your theory is not necessarily the right one, and to ask you to be careful before you affix an indelible brand on a woman who, in my belief, is more sinned against than sinning ! "

" Your theory comes in most opportunely," said the detective, after a thoughtful pause, " and I promise you that I will not be hasty in arresting the suspected party."

" If I am right, Detective Sharpe, all the evidence that may be *hastily* gathered will point toward the woman whom you suspect. If she *is* guilty, she deserves her fate ; but sweep the ground thoroughly before you strike. In the meantime, I give you my personal guarantee that the woman shall remain in her present abode until such time as you are fully satisfied of her guilt or innocence."

" Your assurance relieves me of a great anxiety, and I will spare until the last moment. Only I must do my duty ; I must examine her room——"

" I will help you by taking you to her house. She is probably absent, for I have given orders that she pass the day in the open air. I will not introduce you as a detective, for the reason that she must not be degraded at the present time ; but I will give you ample opportunity to make a thorough search."

"I can ask nothing more!"

"But my liberality will not end there. Keep your eyes and ears open and you will discover the beginning of the path I have cut out for myself. When you have reached the end *after* me, I shall expect your thanks for having prevented you from adding fresh griefs to the grief-burdened life of a misjudged woman."

"You speak positively!"

"And you know that I never speak lightly. All I ask is, that you will exercise your cunning, skill and experience. A false step on your part would probably make me a companion victim to the murdered man. You look incredulous? Wait to the end before you deliver your judgment. I give you my word, Sharpe, that if it were not that I feel my honor engaged in the business, I would leave you here and rush off to the city never to return to this place again!"

"I meekly admit, doctor, that you surprise me. But notwithstanding your doubts, I am proud to believe that you will find in me a valuable aid. I must satisfy myself as to the suspected woman, whom, I frankly confess, you have not entirely cleared in my eyes; but I assure you that no wrong shall come to her through me, until I have first given you my reasons and my intention."

"I repeat your words in saying that I ask nothing better! This is the house; you are a friend of

mine from the city.   That is all that is necessary ;
the rest you may leave to me."

The doctor had whispered this caution before
the front door of Woodbine Villa, the bell of which
he now rang. As he expected, the smiling Miss
Percy appeared in answer to the summons.

"Is Mr. Morris in ? I have met an old friend
from the city whom I am anxious to introduce to
him."

"He is not at home, doctor. He is out with
Miss Gower in the carriage."

"Has she recovered her senses yet ?"

"I fear not ! " was the sad answer.

"If he should return please notify me. Come,
Frank," he said, turning to the detective, "I am at
home in the house of my old friend, and we will
have a smoke and a lounge in my own room."
He loitered behind his friend to whisper to Miss
Percy.

"I will meet you, my dear, in a few minutes on
the veranda."

She nodded and covertly squeezed the doctor's
hand, then vanished into a neighboring room.

The doctor rejoined his friend and both ascended
the stairs. At the top of the first flight, the doctor
pointed significantly with his finger toward a certain door, and continuing his journey, entered a
room on the floor above.

"Stand at this window, Sharpe, and when you
see me conversing with the woman who opened
the door, commence your investigations in the

room indicated. No one is home, and you will not be interrupted. When you have finished, meet me on the veranda."

Miss Percy was waiting for the doctor, and on his appearance rushed to him with a pout.

" I thought you would never come ! "

" You are impatient, my dear ; I have not been in my room above ten minutes. I decoyed my friend into taking off his boots, I forced him into an easy chair, gave him a cigar and unceremoniously left him ? "

" Who is he ? " she asked, boldly.

" A good enough fellow in his way ; but with an unfortunate habit of saving hotel expenses by thrusting himself on his friends. He has been here a week, and discovering that I was in the same village, seized me as a means of extending his acquaintance. I would not have brought him here if I knew Mr. Morris were at home, and I intend to get rid of him before Mr. Morris returns. Have you copied my report ? "

" In my best hand ! "

" You are an angel. But can we not take a little walk under the trees ? "

Miss Percy consented, and having put on her hat the cunning doctor led her away from the house. Under the shadow of the trees the cunning doctor became very communicative. He saddened the woman by informing her that he must soon return to the city to attend to his professional duties and then to his domestic affairs. He was an old bachelor, and his house was at the mercy of careless servants. He was very rich, and it was a temptation. Ah! if he only had a young, energetic and trustworthy housekeeper! If he could obtain the right one, she should receive a large salary and a future of ease and comfort be assured her.

After a certain hesitation, the blushing Miss Percy delicately hinted that she would not be averse to accept the position herself. She had no friends and no claims on her, and her obligations to Miss Gower would end in two weeks and she be free.

The cunning doctor, having stimulated the woman's ambition, now cooled it by announcing that he would think over the matter, and at the earliest opportunity give her the result of his matured thoughts. Miss Percy acquiesced in the inevitable with a sigh, and there was a short silence broken by the woman saying:

"The happy future opened to me makes me forget my present duties. You told me that in her narcotic condition, Miss Gower might do some mischief. Consequently, I have been unusually watchful, and I discovered this pistol under the mattress of her bed."

She handed him a small revolver mounted in silver.

"You are a treasure in every way!" was his enthusiastic comment, as he took the pistol, "and if I can only persuade myself that it will be for your good— But, see, I have forgotten my friend, and he has grown impatient and come for me. Slip into the house, get me your copy of the report, and I will post it, get rid of the bore, and return here as quickly as possible."

Miss Percy smiled, entered the house, but soon reappeared with a long, sealed envelope, which she delivered to the doctor. She watched the two men disappear in the distance with a thoughtful, resolute expression on her handsome face.

" If I could only believe him ! He is vain and foolish, and the thought is a horror ! From house-keeper to wife ! I have conquered greater difficulties, and he is my slave already. If I could only believe him, the bad, evil-minded man ! "

CHAPTER X.

THE doctor and the detective, in the meanwhile, were engaged in an animated conversation

"Did you discover any thing in the room, Sharpe ?"

"Yes ; I found the mull dress, and from the ashes in the grate I raked out a few scraps of the papers that were stolen from me."

"She was foolish not to burn them to the last fragment !" said the doctor, meaningly. "But I suppose she left those scraps to make sure that you would find them !"

"I guess this is the weapon, at last !" said the detective, taking the silver-mounted revolver which the doctor had drawn from his pocket.

"Yes ; and you will notice that one of the chambers is discharged. It is another piece of foolishness on the part of the woman you suspect."

"Miss Percy found it ?"

"Yes ; under the mattress, and innocently brought it to me to take care of."

"She is a tall, graceful woman, doctor !"

"About the same height and build as her mistress," answered the doctor, carelessly, but with a malicious sparkle in his gray eyes.

"A resolute woman," said the detective, thoughtfully.

"My prize, Sharpe! She has consented to become my housekeeper, and I'll wager she is dreaming at this moment of an infatuated old dotard, and the ease with which she can make him her husband, or eat into his fortune by the noble trick of black-mail! The darling! She is greatly interested in poisons, and I allowed her to copy a make-believe report!"

"I will pay her my attentions by and by. Just now I am going to Geoffrey Draper's house. Will you come?"

"No, thank you, I must leave you here and return home."

The doctor parted from the detective with a perplexed, troubled countenance; his shaggy brows were knitted, his lips compressed. Even *his* analytic intellect was troubled.

He lighted a cigar, and with the first puff of smoke his face brightened.

"It is worth while to give these over-praised detectives a lesson. Sharpe is an average specimen of the best, and a pretty muddle I prevented him from producing. I could give them all points!" he thought, warmed by the stimulating glow of egoism. "I suppose the woman-detective for whom I have written is equally stupid. She ought to be here to-day, and at a glance I can read her quali-

ties. It was lucky for them all that Doctor Dubois
was enjoying a vacation in Cypressville ! "

These and similar thoughts removed the last
shadow from the doctor's face, and he reached
Woodbine Villa in excellent spirits.

Mr. Morris had returned ; but Miss Gower had
remained drowsy and silent during the journey.

She was now in her room, reclining on a couch,
attended by the devoted Miss Percy. The maid
was bright, smiling and attractive ; the mistress
dull, passive, preternaturally pale. She lay with
her bright, glassy, staring eyes directed to the ceiling ; her lips were dry ; but a clammy perspiration
oozed from her forehead, and moistened the soft
hair that clung to it. Notwithstanding his brave
assurances, the doctor was anxious, and he sat down
beside the half-conscious woman with a heavy
heart, although he had forced a smile to his face.

" She is wearied by the long ride, doctor," said
Miss Percy, with a pitying glance toward the invalid.

" I fear so, my dear," he answered, absently, " and
I also fear that she has been too cunning for us,
and taken another dose of the vile drug."

" She has not been out of my sight since she
returned."

" Even under your Argus-eyes, my dear, it was
easy enough for her to swallow a pill or two, and
you not be the wiser."

" Can they make laudanum up in pills ? " she
asked, in mild surprise.

" You are not wise in these matters, Miss Percy,

and it is not to be expected you should be. Laudanum is opium in a liquid condition, dissolved in
alcohol ; in its solid form it can be readily made into
pills. Then, again, as morphine, it can be injected
under the skin."

" But it must hurt one terribly to use it in that
way, doctor ! The very idea sets my teeth on edge ! "

" The pain is trifling, and when people are infatuated, like this wretched woman, they do not consider it. But we can easily learn if she has changed
the mode of taking it." While speaking he had
rolled back the loose sleeve of his patient's robe,
and he now gazed at the white, faultless arm with a
sad expression on his face.

" The mark is here, my dear, to condemn her !
To gain speedy forgetfulness, she has used the
hypodermic syringe, and this little puffed up spot
indicates the point where the syringe was pushed
under the skin ! "

Miss Percy studied the spot with much interest.
" She is incorrigible, doctor ; but how was I to
know in my ignorance ? I never heard of the thing
before."

" Of course not ! " said the doctor, kindly. " But
her cunning is only foolishness this time. In her
haste she has forgotten me ! Another day of this
work will kill her ! "

The doctor gazed down at the pale, sunken face,
and was so deeply absorbed in his thoughts that,
for the first time in his life, he paid no attention to
the dinner-bell.

"Dinner is ready," suggested the thoughtful Miss Percy.

"And I am not dressed. But wasn't it the door-bell ? There, listen, it is ringing again."

There could be no doubt of it. The door-bell was rung vigorously, and then there were the sounds of voices in the hall ; especially the loud, laughing voice of a woman.

"It is some visitor, doctor !"

This was the undoubted truth, and a few minutes later, Mr. Morris himself appeared to announce the fact.

"Doctor, one of Miss Gower's friends has, unan-nounced, come here to see her."

"She can not be seen," said the doctor, with affected anger. "Send her about her business ! "

"But she has brought her trunk," answered Mr. Morris, helplessly, "and she means to stay."

"And you needn't put yourself out the least bit on my account !" said a voice in the hall. "I couldn't resist calling on my dear Oriana ! "

A very stylish young lady unceremoniously entered the room, with much rustling of silks, and elaborate sparkle of jewelry. A handsome young lady, self-possessed and graceful, with remarkably bright, piercing black eyes. Mr. Morris introduced the intruder with dismal formality.

"Doctor Dubois, allow me to introduce you to Miss Churchill ; Miss Churchill, Doctor Dubois."

"And is this the dear man whom I have heard so much about," she exclaimed, with shrill volubility.

" Doctor, I am delighted to become acquainted with
you. My friend, Mrs. Pope, is never done speaking about you, and I have been really dying to see
you ! And this young lady ? " she continued, turning to Miss Percy with a smile. " A relation of
yours, Mr. Morris ? "

" No ; Miss Percy, the maid of Miss Gower."

" How very stupid I am, to be sure ! Quite ridiculous ! I am ashamed of myself ! Excuse me.
But really, you mustn't put on ceremonies with me.
I saw, as I came by, that the dinner was on the
table. I have dined, and I couldn't touch another
mouthful ! I shall feel perfectly at home here,
and I hope you won't let the soup get cold on *my*
account ? when dear Oriana wakes she will show me
my room, and we shall get on lovely ! "

Mr. Morris shrugged his shoulders, and, as he
turned to leave with the doctor, beckoned to Miss
Percy.

" She acts already as if she owns the house,"
said the doctor, " and if she does not talk us all
to death we are lucky ! "

" What can I do, Dubois ? She is an old friend.
I told her Miss Gower was ill, but I could not send
her back to her home three hundred miles away !
May I ask you, Miss Percy, to have the blue-room
made ready for the bold invader ? I am sorry to
trouble you ; but she came so unexpectedly that
she has put me at my wit's end."

" There is no trouble, Mr. Morris," answered
Miss Percy, graciously ; " a little dusting and a

little arranging and all is ready. Pardon me if I suggest that the dinner is getting cold, while the young lady seems fully able to take care of herself."

"Miss Percy speaks like an angel!" said the doctor. "I *am* hungry, Morris, too hungry to change my attire ; and the wordy young lady *is* fully able to take care of herself."

The young lady in question vindicated these encomiums ; for when Mr. Morris visited her after dinner he discovered that she had changed her traveling attire for a gorgeous full evening dress, and she was sitting in her friend's room in smiling content, amusing herself by turning over the pages of a fashion-book.

The doctor had gone in search of Miss Percy, who, he discovered, had betaken herself to her own apartment. He sent a message, which brought her to the library, with a frown on her fair face.

"You are out of humor, my dear ?"

"Miss Churchill would provoke a saint! She takes me for a servant, and amused herself with ordering me about, until I gave her to understand my true position."

"Mr. Morris tells me that she is the daughter of a farmer who suddenly became rich. She is anxious to dazzle an old friend with her gorgeous attire, and her knowledge of the world picked up in a few months' travel in Europe. I gave you credit for more discernment, my dear. She is only one of the vulgar rich, not worth a sensible woman's anger !"

" She is very aggravating ! "

" She is very rich, and that, in the eyes of most people, would excuse her."

" She asked me if my mistress had not taken just a little too much champagne, as it always affected her in that way ! "

" And most of her life she has drank nothing but cider and weak elderberry wine ! She will become tired of this quiet little place before the week is out."

" Not more tired than I am. It is a dull, tiresome hole ! "

" The shoddy woman has put you out of humor with it."

" I hated it from the first. I shall leave it when my quarter's services are ended," she said, determinedly.

" You have positively decided ? "

" Positively, sir ! I have made up my mind to follow you, even if you change yours."

"Am I so fickle ? "

" You are a man, and you will forget me when you have turned your back on the village."

"Never ! " he answered seriously.

" You only look on me as a higher species of servant," she persisted.

" Ah, my dear, and can you read my heart ? "

" I know my own ! " she said, sadly, " and I know that having sunk to the degradation of a servant, I can never again rise to the station in which I was born ! "

"If I did not know better, my dear, I should say that you are in love?"

"Is it a crime?"

"No; a merit in a pretty young woman like you! An old man like me can only look on and sigh with envy."

"You are *not* old," she said, impetuously, "and if you were, what has love to do with such matters? You are wise and you are good, while the young of your sex are foolish and wicked."

"You flatter me, my dear!"

"If you knew me better you would not say so."

"You are very amiable, child!"

"Child!" she repeated hotly, "I am a woman; free to do as I like; to love where I will; to offer my life, my soul, to him I love. Oh, if you were less wise and more human! You can never have loved!"

The situation was becoming dangerous and yet very attractive! The doctor was exercising his diplomacy, and his gallantry at the same time. Unfortunately he did not hear the approaching footsteps in the hall, while Miss Percy's senses were sharper than his own.

"You will teach me, my dear!" he said, while putting a fatherly arm around her waist.

He drew her toward him, and, intensely amused by his own cunning, kissed her on the forehead. It was fine gallantry, and the tableau was charming; but it surprised Mr. Morris, who stood at the doorway, and announced his presence with a discreet little cough.

At the sound Miss Percy flushed a deep crimson, rose, put her hands to her face, and rushed out of the room ; the doctor, a picture of confusion, resting motionless on the lounge.

" You are coming it strong in your old age, Dubois !" said Mr. Morris, with a chuckle.

"She is a little fiend !" answered the doctor, drawing a long breath. " Willing to compromise herself to get me in her power ! "

" She is a mighty pretty maiden, Dubois ; may I congratulate you on your conquest ? "

" If you knew all, Morris, you would be more serious ; and if Miss Churchill does not relieve me soon, I will strangle the little devil with my own hands."

Miss Churchill was seemingly more intent on making herself at home than in troubling herself with the doctor's affairs. She insolently ordered Miss Percy from the sick woman's room, expressing the intention of attending herself on her friend. She closed the door after the indignant maid and locked it, shrieking through the key-hole that *she* " didn't want any poke-noses around ! "

This done, she seated herself near the table, reading from a book of poetry. From time to time she consulted her watch ; at a certain hour she rose and approached the bed on which her wretched friend tossed and moaned in a semiconscious state. She opened a little hand-bag, took from it a bottle and a spoon, and poured a spoonful of the bottle's contents down her friend's throat. Pausing a moment, and with her intelligent eyes carefully watching the result, she repeated the dose. The restlessness of the patient was stilled, and she sunk into a placid sleep. A condition of things that had not obtained for many days.

Miss Churchill again returned to her book of poetry. Near midnight she dropped into what seemed to be a deep sleep, and snored with a vigor that told well for her health. Before plunging into unconsciousness she had, with rustic caution, turned off the gas, and the room was in shadow, save for a few arrows of moonlight that struggled through the half-closed blinds.

Had she been awake, she would have heard the rustling of a woman's dress in the hall without, and a light hand turning the handle of the door. But Miss Churchill slept like a farmer's daughter, and her unromantic snoring maintained its rhythm with the regularity of a piece of classic poetry.

A hand, or an instrument, was now busied with the key outside ; there was a sharp, metallic click, and the door itself was softly opened, and a pair of bright eyes glanced into the room. The bed was in shadow, but a ray of moonlight fell on the lounge and revealed a woman's form stretched out at full length.

The door opened wider, and a figure glided silently into the room, paused a moment near the lounge, and then, with noiseless feet, approached the bed and leaned over it. At the same instant there was a flash of brilliant light as from an electric arc, a dazzling light that blazed in the intruder's face, and caused her to start back with a little shriek. She turned instinctively toward the lounge, but the figure on it still lay motionless, snoring with classic regularity. The light-flash was only momentary; it blazed up and then expired, leaving the room in its original gloom.

The intruder stood for a moment the victim of fear and perplexity; her heart beat violently, and there was a tremor in the usually firm lips and hands. She did not again approach the bed, but retired from the room with the same noiselessness with which she entered it. When the door closed behind her, Miss Churchill ceased snoring and quickly rose from the lounge. In an incredibly short space of time she had cast aside her outer silken garment, beneath which was a simple dress of an inconspicuous color and fashion. She now seized a bonnet, to which a wig was attached, and pulled it down over her soft black hair, arranging her toilet in the dark as skillfully as if she were standing before a mirror in a full blaze of light. She then opened the door and peered anxiously out into the hall. As if in answer to some mysterious summons, the doctor, in shoeless feet, entered the room.

"I have given her the medicine, doctor," said Miss Churchill, in a whisper, "and she is sleeping

well. Your electric light was also a success ; in
all probability it saved a life. Wait my return
here ! "

She left the room, glided down the stairs, passed
through a window that she opened in the library,
and crouched in the shadow of the veranda, near
the front door. Strange as the house must have
been to her, she never hesitated in her actions, but
moved about as if she had lived in the building
since childhood and knew every one of its angles.
But even her haste indicated deliberation and forethought ; astonishing qualities in a farmer's
daughter and a woman of fashion ! She crouched
in the darkness as if the part of spy were the business of her life. Her patience was as remarkable
as her calmness ; she remained for a long time as
motionless as a statue, and when the door opened
not even a sigh of relief escaped her. After an
interval, she followed the figure that had cautiously
made its exit from the house, and which was now
speeding along in the shadow of the bushes ; the
figure of a woman, running, rather than walking, as
if goaded onward by her own troubled thoughts.
Her road led her in the direction of the old house
in which the murder was committed, and she never
paused in her journey until she reached its boundary walls. Here her footsteps stopped, and she
glanced up at the gloomy building that seemed
floating in an ocean of mist ! The pursuing Miss
Churchill also paused, with eyes directed toward
the cupola, from which issued a light, the only

evidence of life in the dreary building. The light flashed, disappeared, flashed again and then mysteriously vanished. The figure standing in the moonlight paused irresolutely, and uttered an exclamation of disappointment. It then turned its back on the house and for a short distance retraced its steps. It rested for a moment beneath a huge tree that overhung the roadside, and its hands seemed gliding over the gnarled, scaly trunk. It came out into the light again bearing a paper in its hand, which it opened and read in the moon's rays. It tore a fragment from the paper, seemingly wrote on it with a pencil, after which it returned to the tree. When it again reappeared, it continued its journey uninterruptedly to the house from which it had emerged. Miss Churchill followed until the door of Woodbine Villa closed behind it, when she retraced her steps in the direction of the mysterious old tree. The distance she had to walk was over a half-mile, and the object she sought was surrounded by hundreds of similar companions, but she walked toward it in a bee-line, never hesitating, never pausing, never swerving from the straight line. Reaching the tree, she, in turn, ran her hands lightly over the trunk ; but she discovered nothing ; no suggestive projection, no cavity, nothing indicating the trysting place of lovers, or of knaves. Perplexed, yet with energy unabated, she renewed her search. Higher up the trunk, just within reach of her outstretched arm, the branches diverged, and in the angle thus formed there was an old bird's-nest of the last year. Miss Churchill was interested in this object, and in the midst of the dry grass, and mud and feathers, her exploring hand discovered a scrap of paper. This she eagerly seized, and, thanks to the bright moonlight, mastered a portion of its contents. On one side, written in a woman's handwriting, were the words: "*Danger! Spies! Must see you! To-morrow noon!*" On the other were a few disjointed words written by a man. It was the fragment of a short note, and was meaningless in its present condition. Miss Churchill's sharp eyes deciphered the words: "*to the end——with my life!—double the price!—desert and hang!*"

After much hesitation, Miss Churchill restored the paper to the strange retreat from which she had abstracted it. Before retiring she again glanced toward the old house. To her astonishment, the light was flashing from the cupola with steady, uninterrupted brightness. No! it appeared and vanished in the old way! Three flashes, then darkness! five flashes, then darkness; one flash, then darkness, and so on, with a certain regularity in its irregularity. It was evidently a series of signals or of words; but to whom? Was the cupola of Woodbine Villa within sight of the cupola yonder? Miss Churchill could ask, but she could not answer, the question. From her position on the ground she saw nothing but the tree-tops tossed about in the chill night wind. But even while speculating, the light vanished and did not reappear. She waited with praiseworthy patience, but an hour passed and the mysterious signals were not repeated. For the present, at least, patience was not to bring its reward. Miss Churchill, however, bore her disappointment with uncomplaining philosophy, and retraced her steps toward the house in which she was a temporary guest. Reaching the grounds which surrounded the villa, she instinctively glanced upward toward the roof of the house. There was no light in the cupola that rested in shadowy darkness against the moonlighted sky.

CHAPTER XI.

A LECTURE AND A SURPRISE.

A MOONLIGHT night had dissolved into a cheerless morning ; a cold, drizzling rain poured down from a gray mist above into a brown mist below. The view even from the windows of Woodbine Villa was not cheerful ; it gave Miss Percy the blues, and, ordinarily, she was a young woman of great elasticity of nature, and with an abundance of happy, animal vitality. In the early dawn she had drawn aside the curtain from before one of her bed-room windows, expecting to find cheerfulness in a flood of warm sunlight, only to discover the clouds weeping grimy tears on the windows, with a wearisome rhythm that suggested a funeral march. The trunks of the fruit-trees had turned from a silver gray to a flaring brown, and the shrill wind tore off their spotted leaves and spotted fruit with deserved contempt. The lawns were converted into little lakes, and the roadways into bogs. Over yonder, a diseased branch of a pear tree had been twisted from the healthier living tissue, and it hung by the bark only, swaying to and fro like a human body held in a hempen rope ! The flower-beds had lost their attractiveness, sug-

gesting a grave-yard rather than a pleasure ground.
A most wretched day, surely ; the soaked ground
littered with withered leaves, the rain drearily
pattering against the window-panes, and the wind
shrieking its mockery in unexpected spasms.

And the looking-glass brought no better consolation. The Miss Percy reflected in it had no color
in her usually rosy cheeks ; her eyes were heavy and
dull, and her general appearance listless and
moody. A little dab of rouge on either cheek, a
judicious touch of chalk here and there, improved
matters ; but it could not be denied that Miss
Percy was under the influence of the weather, and,
in addition, looked as if she had passed a sleepless and wretched night.

She devoted unusual time and care to her toilet ;
her hair was arranged in its most becoming manner,
and the white rose with a faint flush of red was a
charming contrast to its raven blackness. As if to
defy the chill, damp weather, she wore a white dress
of some thin material, through which the warm flesh
of her arms and shoulders could be faintly seen.
A white rose nestled at her throat, held in its place
by a curiously-carved silver breast-pin.

This labor of love finished, she studied herself in
the mirror with critical severity. She admitted
that the costume was somewhat unseasonable ; but,
at the same time, conscientiously granted that it
was very attractive.

As neither vanity nor criticism could suggest any
thing further, she again approached the window,

and wearied herself with the dull landscape. To
her left, a recently added extension of the house
interfered with her view ; but she seemed to find
more interest in the work of the builder than in the
works of nature, especially in a window that was
almost diagonally opposite, and on a lower level
than her own. She watched this window with great
interest, and when its curtain was withdrawn, and
a ruddy-faced man in a dressing-gown stared out
into the rain, she tapped on the window-pane and
kissed her hand. The ruddy-faced man nodded,
smiled, and opened his window.

Miss Percy left her room, passed through the
narrow hallway, and, descending a few steps,
traversed another hall, and finally stopped before a
door, on which she lightly tapped. The door was
opened, and the ruddy face and little figure of the
doctor were revealed.

" I want to speak with you very seriously, doctor !
May I come in ? "

" Let us go down to the sitting-room."

" I do not wish to be seen or interrupted."

" It is still early, my child, and we have a full
hour before the indolent people here make their
appearance."

" We were disturbed yesterday," she said, hesitat-
ingly, and with shrinking modesty, " and I have felt
humiliated ever since. Not for myself," she
added, with a happy, retrospective smile, " but for
you. It shall not happen again. I am very sorry—
also for you ! "

Despite his embarrassed resistance, she had entered the room, leaving the door open, and she now approached him and placed a pleading hand on his arm.

Unfortunately, a sleepy eyed maid-servant passed along the hall at this moment, and, after staring into the room, tripped hastily down the stairs, with a look of horror and amazement on her face.

Fortunately, the affectionate Miss Percy was ignorant of this little incident, her back being turned to the door ; but the doctor was less lucky, and what he saw brought the perspiration to his forehead.

" You should be more discreet," he said, suppressing his anger with an effort. " One of the servants has seen you in my room,· and this little business will be the talk of the house ! "

" If I am satisfied, sir, have you any right to complain ? " she asked, with charming audacity. " I wish to tell you, my good adviser, something about that horrible Miss Churchill. I believe she drinks ! "

" I hope not."

" You shall hear. She ordered me out of the room ; played the part of maid to Miss Gower in a very bungling manner, and, if you will forgive my boldness, acted in a very coarse, unladylike way. I was worried and could not sleep until I had assured myself of your patient's comfort. About twelve o'clock I tapped on the door. No one answered me, and all I heard was a very vigorous

snore from Miss Churchill, and moans from the
neglected Miss Gower. I forced my way into
the room ; the gas was turned off, but Miss Gower
was groaning as if in great pain, and her friend
was sleeping on the lounge. The foolish woman
believes that all the people here are bent on
ruining her friend, physically and morally, and
before going to sleep had surrounded her with
electric wires. At any rate, when I touched her
an electric light flared up at the head of the bed,
and sent my heart into my throat. I was never
before so startled in my life ! "

"It's a wonder our rustic friend did not sur-
round herself with the same safeguard ! "

"I am not concerned with the foolishness, sir ;
but I will not share the responsibility with that
woman. If you wish to engage me I am content ;
but in any case I will not remain here."

"Are you serious ?" asked the doctor, with unaf-
fected surprise.

"Make the offer to take me to the city by the
next train, and test me. I am utterly indifferent
to the opinions of the world. Take me away from
this place and its degradations."

There could be no doubt of Miss Percy's earn-
estness, and it took away the doctor's breath and
robbed his scientific theory of the crime of the
larger amount of its value.

"I cannot leave Miss Gower in her illness," he
said, after a pause, "and I shall not *run* away from
you and your trust. You must have patience.

Keep away from Miss Gower, and leave her in the charge of her ridiculous friend. I will think what is best to be done."

" Is it your wish that I should remain ?"

" Yes, my child, for the present, at least."

" I will obey *you*," she said, restraining a strong inclination to laugh in his face. "I will try and be patient and obedient for *your* sake. Forgive me for taking up so much of your valuable time, and think of me as a wretched woman, who would accept torture if it would add to your happiness."

She smiled at him—a sad, wan smile—waved her hand, and left him to his perplexities.

He was unusually quiet at breakfast, and unusually surprised after breakfast. Captain Travers had retired to smoke his cigar in the open air, in defiance of the rain, and the doctor was about to follow his example, when Mr. Morris said :

" One moment, Dubois ; I am in the mood to give you a lecture."

" That will be original, Morris, and amusing."

" It seems to me, Dubois, that we are all a party of originals. But let us come to the point : what are you doing to Miss Percy ?"

" Doing ?" asked the doctor, in surprise.

" Yes, doing ! I heard the servants talking about seeing her in your bed-room this morning. I ain't a grim moralist, as you know; but isn't it coming it just a trifle strong ? It isn't fair, Dubois, because you think that the young lady is a guilty wretch, that you should take advantage of her trust in you, by robbing her of her character. Hang me, if you are even discreet in the business ! ''

" You are surely joking ! '' gasped the doctor.

" It is confoundedly funny, and when I first heard of it I laughed myself into a species of apoplectic fit. But coming down to sober facts, it isn't a thing to be proud of. If science has these privileges, I intend to become a doctor at the earliest opportunity.''

" You are perversely ignorant,'' said the doctor, angrily. " Do you know what I have saved your niece from ? ''

" Poison ? ''

" No, jail ! She is suspected of having murdered the man Addison. Sharpe would have arrested her but for me.''

" And Sharpe is an idiot ! '' retorted Mr. Morris, indignantly. " I'm not prejudiced in Oriana's favor, but I'd sooner believe *I* perpetrated the crime than she. You're a theorist, Dubois, and recently you have honored me with some very profound disquisitions on hypodermic injections, guilty maids, and your own virtues. I've got a theory, too, and that is, the young woman Percy is deeply smitten with your beauty, and that if she drugged my niece she drugged her out of jealousy. She has shown a great deal of attention to you, you must admit.''

" I can not deny it, but——''

" Put it to the test. If, as you suspect, the little maid is connected with the murder, and if her safety depends, as you again suspect, on narcotizing or killing my niece, she will cling to her place here with a desperation proportionate to her danger. If she is only acting from jealousy, she will willingly leave, provided you bear her company. Make her the offer and test her."

" It is needless," said the doctor, with a troubled face. " She has already consented to go with me."

" Poor little thing ! And you play with her the part of Zoilus and Sardanapalus at the same time ; and at your age, too ! "

" I deny your insinuation," said the doctor, hotly. " I am guiltless of even the intention of wrong. You would do better to defend the relation rather than the stranger."

" I have greater respect for the stranger ! " answered Mr. Morris, with unruffled calmness. " I have the honor of being related to Oriana's family; I keep up with them an occasional correspondence, though I have not seen any of them since I left England a boy, now some thirty years ago. I receive a letter, within comparatively recent times, in which I am begged to look after a young lady who was born after I left the country of my birth, and whom, consequently, I have never seen. I am told that the people who have adopted her are dead. Honored with these meager facts, I am directed to go to Cypressville and look her up. I purchase a house in the village at the same time, and I determine, quietly, to examine matters on my own account. I find the young lady has quarreled with the young man to whom she was engaged—I don't

admire her, but killing him is out of the question !
—I find that she is in very questionable relations
with another man. Is she guilty? It is none of
my business to inquire; in fact, I prefer to remain in
ignorance on that point. I go to her, tell her I am
her relation, and invite her to live in my house. I
tell her that, if she accepts my offer, she must break
off all her village friendships ; that she will be well
cared for, receive something on my death, but must
not expect a gushing devotion which I do not feel.
I tell her I am willing to bury her past life, whatever
it may have been, and ask no questions. I tell
her she must begin a new life, and that I will remain
a placid uncle as long as she behaves herself. She
flashes up indignantly ; I turn on my heel, and tell
her I will call for the answer on the morrow. I
call, and she becomes a member of my household.
Had I been more curious, or less eccentric—"

"Say indifferent ! " interrupted the doctor.

"I accept the amendment ! Had I been less
indifferent, Miss Gower might have had a less
pleasant home. But I have received her without
comment, and if she has not kept to the strict letter
of her promise, she has again to thank my indifference that she has not been turned into the streets.
That is my relationship with my very charming relative. If she is innocent of all wrong, so much the
better for her ; if she has forgotten herself, so much
the worse ; but, in either case, I am profoundly
ignorant. That she would commit a murder under
any circumstances, I would not believe if the entire

world swore to it ; and to defend her from the vile charge I would spend my money to the last copper. As to the rest, I am silent !"

"And yet you allow Captain Travers to fall in love with her, and perhaps marry her ! "

"I am not Captain Travers's guardian ! If he is foolish enough to marry, he must take the jump blindly, like the rest of his sex. I know nothing, and I do not intend to play the part of spy for the very amiable captain. If he wants my niece, he is welcome to her ; if he is in a critical mood, he must use the microscope himself. If he does not marry her, she remains here, and the world goes on just the same."

" But surely you do not think—" began the doctor.

" Pardon me, Dubois, I don't think any thing, except the one thing you are trying to sneak away from. You have cunningly dragged me away from the subject, and it is like your scientific hypocrisy. *My* nerves are not high-strung, but, even looking at the worst side, *I* could not treacherously win the affections and receive the kisses of a woman whom I meant to fling on the gallows."

" You describe the case too coarsely."

" That's the gist of it, and fine words won't alter it. The girl Percy has no reason, except love, for humbling herself before you. She warms your slippers ; she goes in the kitchen to cook you delicacies ; she places little bouquets in your room. You are a wretch, Dubois! But the sermon's ended, and I leave you to digest it at your leisure!"

Like all good sermons, only a portion of it was digested—that portion which agreed with the hearer's prejudices and vanity. The doctor admitted to himself that the maid might do worse than fall in love with him; but that his theory was wrong!

The appearance of Miss Churchill, in a wonderful morning-robe, recalled him to the hard, prosaic world again. He exchanged a formal bow with her; but it was not until her late breakfast had been served, and the servant dismissed, that he ventured to speak to her.

"How is our patient?"

"Weak, but, I think, rational."

"Has she spoken yet?"

"A few words; but before the morning is over I think she will be able to tell all you wish to know—that is, if you do not wish to know too much. Tonics and change of scene will do the rest."

"Is she aware of the nature of her illness?"

"I think she has lost all idea of time. She talks of croquet, and of a Captain Travers, whom she is very anxious to see."

"Did you leave her alone?"

"No; a servant is with her, arranging the room. I have left orders that she shall remain there until my return. Now, in turn, doctor, let me ask, do you think that opium was the only drug used?"

"I am strongly of the belief, Miss Churchill, that it was used only as a mask for something more

hurtful, if that is possible.   The attempt was on the
brain, to fill it with fancies that would help the
plotters in their diabolical scheme.   She was to have
seen frightful visions, and her wild horror at the fancies was to have impressed others as remorse for a
murderous crime."

"Diabolical, doctor, surely ; but she is saved
from that wretchedness, at least ! "

"My task has not been easy, Miss Churchill, to
conceal my own suspicions and to do justice to our
patient at the same time.   Her nervous system is
at a very low point of vitality, and I hope you will
remember this.   Any sudden shock may not only
interfere with the course of justice, but hopelessly
ruin our patient's constitution.   For the present,
news from the outside world must be carefully kept
away from her.   At least, until we can offer surety
instead of doubt."

"I am persuaded, doctor, that in a few days
surety will be reached.   I have no doubt—what is
that ? " she asked, suddenly starting to her feet.

A wild, shrill shriek, repeated again and again—a
shriek that drove the color from the doctor's face,
and thrilled the nerves of even the unimpressionable
Miss Churchill !

The doctor expressed the idea of both in his
startled exclamation :

"Miss Gower ! "

He rushed up-stairs closely followed by the woman.

There could be no doubt as to the cause of the
wild cry ; it was repeated in their presence by the

figure tossing about on the bed, with its hands clutching at its hair. Wild, piercing shrieks! A servant stood staring in amazement, a shattered goblet at her feet.

"What is the meaning of this?" asked Miss Churchill, imperiously.

"I'm sure I don't know!" answered the servant, grasping, unconsciously, at her own throat as if from it the cries were coming.

"Did you leave the room?"

"She asked me for a glass of cold water, a kind o' wild like! I went to git it, and when I came back she was a screaming and tearing herself!"

At these words the doctor, with an oath, rushed from the room, speeded up a flight of stairs and impetuously pushed open a door.

Miss Percy was in dishabille, her perfect shoulders and arms were uncovered, and she was busied in arranging her loose, flowing hair. She started at the intrusion, flushed from brow to bosom, stared angrily—and then smiled!

"You are welcome, doctor," she said gayly; "only, before you come in, please remember that I have not suggested this indiscretion!"

"Pardon me," he stammered.

"I am glad you have come," she said, with a fine seriousness. "I was puzzled, and your advice will be welcome. Resolve my doubts by answering this very important question: in what way shall I arrange my hair?"

The handsome face was still turned toward him,

with smiling lips, but with an angry glow in the dark eyes. He reproached himself more for his unjust suspicion than for his unpardonable indiscretion.

" I heard a shriek of pain," he said, excusing himself with a weak falsehood, "and I thought it came from this room. Pardon me ! "

He closed the door, and descended the stairs, angrily cursing his own impetuosity.

The shrieks had ceased when he entered his patient's room ; but she was still tossing about on the bed, uttering low, convulsive moans. Once she started to a sitting position, stared wildly yet pleadingly around, groaning :

" I am innocent ! I am innocent ! " Then the voice was raised to a shriek, " Save me ! Save me ! " and then sank into a dreary moan.

Miss Churchill had turned a questioning face toward the doctor as he entered, and he replied to it in words :

" Not possible ! She was not in a condition to leave her room !" To hide his blushes he approached the bed.

" Then, doctor, we can only suppose, that on returning to her senses, she recalls a fact which she must have known before."

" Or," said a calm voice at the door, " remembers an act which she committed in a passion, and to drive which from her mind she indulged in an overdose of poison !"

The doctor turned, to meet the half smiling, half mocking face of Detective Sharpe !

CHAPTER XII.

MISS CHURCHILL ON THE TRAIL.

THE detective stood quietly at the door while the doctor attended to his patient, amusing himself with noting the contents of the room, especially the one object that he had not before seen, the busy, yet calm, Miss Churchill. In a short time, thanks to the doctor's skill, the restlessness of the patient was subdued, and she sunk into silence, and an unconsciousness that simulated sleep.

At this favorable moment the detective asked : " Can I have a short conversation with you, doctor, down-stairs ? "

" We will converse here, Sharpe ! " said the doctor ; then, in answer to the cautioning glance, he added : " Allow me, Detective Sharpe, to introduce to you Miss Churchill, an old friend of Miss Gower, to whom I have given all my confidence, and on whom I depend as on myself ! "

The detective bowed and shrugged his shoulders ; he had no confidence in young women ; but that was the doctor's look-out.

" As you like, doctor. I came, in the first place, to tell you of some little items I have picked up, and then to ask for your company. Miss Churchill will pardon me if my words tell hard against her friend."

"She won't believe them, nevertheless," said that young lady, pertly. "I never did have much belief in you detectives, even in novels. If the authors didn't go out of their way to make you right at the last moment, you'd go on the wrong track even there!"

"I hope you are right, Miss Churchill! But, doctor, the facts are these: one of the results of my labors yesterday was to discover that Miss Gower was the woman who so frequently visited Mr. Draper's house; I have witnesses to prove this, and also to prove that Miss Gower was seen in conversation with Mr. Draper at eleven o'clock on the morning of the murder; and they acted toward each other as if they were engaged in a violent quarrel. I have traced Mr. Draper, up to that hour, in this village, when he is suddenly lost. These are *facts,* doctor."

"I will accept them as such, Sharpe!"

"Well, then, I will go to another matter. Do you remember the tramp who was caught plundering the fruit trees in the dead man's grounds? I mean Ralph Price, who saw the mysterious woman enter and come out of the house?"

"I remember the excellent man!"

"Well, he has been in charge of one of my men ever since. Yesterday I again put his nose to the grindstone, with the determination to find out all he knows. He finally admitted that Miss Gower was the woman whom he had seen."

" Did he name her ? "

" Yes ; it seems that several times he had visited Mr. Morris's house on begging missions ; and that once he had gone on an errand for the young lady herself. He mentioned her by name as the original of the lady he had previously described."

" Why did he not give her name at first ? "

" Well, she had been kind to him ; and seeing me, a public officer, very interested in the matter, he thought I meant her harm, and so pretended ignorance of her name. However, threats of long imprisonment loosened his tongue, and restored his memory ! "

" Where is he now ? "

" Where he has always been, in charge of one of my men."

" Where is he confined ? "

" In the jail here."

" I suppose, then, I can see him ? "

" Not without an order from me. That is, not to speak to him. I gave the people the order, so that he might not be tampered with."

" Will you write me an order."

" Willingly," said the detective, with a smile, and writing in his pocket-book. " Here is the order, doctor, and I am anxious to hear what science will make out of this very troublesome admission."

" Are there any other facts ? "

" One more. I have discovered that Mr. Tom Merton has taken a steamer for Europe. He spoke freely to his friends before going, with this result : the rich relative from whom he has so many expectations largely invested *his* money in the African diamond fields and other shaky speculations. These have collapsed ; Mr. Merton finds that he is ruined, with many other foolish speculators, and rushes away, in hopes that something may be saved. I am satisfied that he may be excluded, henceforth, from the line of our investigations. If you still doubt, I will surrender to your criticism the large number of details that my agents have gathered together on this point."

"I may take advantage of your kindness later. What else ? "

"Nothing, except Mr. Newton intends to bury his master to-day. Strangely enough, none of the people here have shown much interest in following the murdered man to his last home. Mr. Terms is going, and to exhaust that's man's information I have consented to accompany him. Thinking you might like to share my pleasure, I have come to invite you."

"I can not leave the house to-day," said the doctor, after glancing at Miss Churchill.

"And I can not spare more time to this pleasant company," said the detective, rising. "And let me say, Doctor Dubois, if you do not very quickly give me some positive reason to the contrary, I shall be compelled to follow my original intention and end my duties by arresting Miss Gower. I am sorry to say it, but I think I am in possession of enough facts to justify me in my line of conduct."

" She is in no danger of escaping," answered the doctor, with a glance at the bed. " But I am still in hopes of convincing you of your error."

" Before retiring, allow me to explain to Miss Churchill that my strange appearance here is due to Mr. Morris. He opened the door for me, or, rather, he was going out as I was coming in, and he sent me here. I say so much," he added, with a smile, " that Miss Churchill may not confound me with those wonderful detectives who appear and disappear with such supernatural mystery."

Miss Churchill listened to the explanation in languid indifference ; but when he disappeared she started into sudden activity.

" He is tiresome as well as foolish," she said, rising, and with a reassuring nod to the depressed doctor. " Please give me the order he has written, and while I am away, personally attend to the case of your patient."

" You are not then discouraged ? "

" I have successfully emerged from greater difficulties. You all have tried your hands, and it is time now for me to try mine ! "

" And what is your real opinion ? "

" I have none, doctor, until I reach the end of my journey. The people who talk discover nothing but paradoxes. Let me then act and keep silent."

She retired to her own room, changed her showy robe for a sedate walking-dress and bonnet, and then sat down and patiently waited. After a short time passed in this idleness, she rose, seized an umbrella, and passing down the stairs left the house. The direction in which she first walked was toward the railway station, and reaching this cheerless little place, she became a part of the dozen or more people who were waiting for the expected train. The rain fell heavily, and, as she had no water-proof, and her dress was lavender-colored and of light material, she retired into the moldy, deserted room that was reserved for the use of her sex. She re-appeared as the train was thundering toward the station and the passengers were rushing down the steps to meet it. But in the interval her black hair had turned to reddish brown ; the greater portion of her body was protected by a water-proof garment, and the line of dress that was visible had faded from lavender into black. Her face had un_dergone a more remarkable change ; and even her delicate little umbrella had become converted into an unwieldy blue anomaly that defied classification. She did not enter the train ; but, when it had passed on, she struck across the fields in a direction directly opposite to her former course. So long as she was in the inhabited region, she maintained a steady, sedate walk ; but when she reached the woodlands, she drew the cap of her water-proof over her head and face, closed her umbrella, and passed onward with light and rapid steps.

It was a dreary, uncomfortable journey, over soaked fields, boggy roads, and under dripping trees ; with the wind shrieking angrily and flinging

rain that was as cold as ice directly in her face.
But there was no rest in the determined steps, no
relaxation in the tireless energy, until the old house
loomed through the gloom and rain, like a black
blot against the less black sky. At this point of
her journey, she paused, and became deeply interested in studying the situation of the mansion.
Its picturesqueness was charming ; the grounds
must have been, at one time, very attractive ; the
ocean view was grand ; the stone walls and iron
gratings surrounding the extensive domain must
have cost large sums of money, for the stone was
of rare quality, carefully polished and cut, and as
accurately laid as the walls of a house. But these
items did not interest Miss Churchill ; she was
deeply absorbed in studying a dense mass of trees
that were some feet distant from the boundary line
of the property ; and which suggested mystery and
doubt to her fine instinct. Much might be accomplished in the gloom of these trees, and they so
faced an angle of the house that they could not be
seen from its windows. She studied these natural
objects with the eye of an educated critic, and was
not greatly surprised when she saw something moving in the midst of them. She glanced toward the
house ; not a sign of life was visible at the windows
or in the grounds surrounding it. Nothing but
desolation and a monotonous downpour of rain.
She again glanced toward the trees ; the moving
object had vanished ; but on one of the tree-
branches a narrow strip of gray cloth fluttered

wildly in the wind. And now from the woods above
her there glided a human figure draped from head
to foot in a water-proof cloak. The figure sped
over the ground, entered the clump of trees, gradually diminished in height, and then vanished.
After a moment of thought, Miss Churchill followed in the wake of the vanished figure, and, in
turn, entered the mysterious little grove, which
consisted of trees so closely planted that their
branches touched and intermingled overhead.
The ground beneath was bare of grass, and in its
midst was a large stone that was strangely suggestive of druidical rites and ceremonies. A decep-
tive stone as to weight, for, with an effort, even the
slight Miss Churchill could raise it backward on
its large steel hinges. Without stopping to take
note of this fact, or to bless a long-dead old man
for his eccentricities, she boldly descended the
flight of rugged steps, that seemed built in the
ground, and as she descended allowed the decep-
tive stone to close over her. She found herself in
a dark, damp, narrow passage-way, hardly broader
than her own shoulders. The air was heavy, but,
to her surprise, it was not stifling ; and, with her
hands touching the walls on either side, she walked
forward cautiously, but unhesitatingly. She soon
found herself in a broad, gloomy vault, lighted by
one narrow, barred window in the wall above. To
her left was a flight of narrow, winding steps, and
these she ascended till the sound of voices and an
increase of light indicated that, for the present,

she had ventured far enough. She seated herself
on the steps, glanced upward to the half-opened
door on a line with the top of her head, and listened to the conversation that reached her as if it
were being delivered through an imperfect speaking tube. The voices revealed that a man and a
woman were speaking ; the man in deep, angry
tones ; the woman in the most musical of voices.

"You are always making mountains out of mole-
hills!" were the first words that reached her ears.
"If that is all you have to tell, I knew it already,
and a pretty waste of time when I most need it!
Is that all?"

"No, it is not all, and I order you, Max Newton,
to take a lower tone with me or you'll repent it!"

"Curse you for an idiot! What *do* you want?"

"To bid you farewell ; I'm going away."

"Is this a time for jest?" asked the man's voice,
sternly.

"I'm in sober earnest. I'm going away, to-day,
to-morrow, or next day; but I go just the same."

"If I allow you!"

"You can't help yourself."

"Move a step without my permission and take
the consequences!"

"I am not afraid. To hang me would be to
hang yourself, and I am very easy so far as you are
concerned!"

"If I thought you were in earnest," came the
somber answer, "I would dash out your worthless
brains against the stone wall on which you are

leaning. Speak plainly. Are you dissatisfied? If your miserly soul craves for money, tell me how much would stifle your complaints?"

" I am dissatisfied with every thing. You took advantage of my necessities to drag me into the vile business—— "

" I knew your soul almost as well as you knew it yourself!"

" You dog! My hands and soul were clean until you tempted me! Starvation and degradation on one side; comparative wealth and crime on the other. I *was* starving, I saw only the food and grasped it. I am less wicked than I hoped to be. You have sunk me to hell with your temptations, but you shall not rob me of all happiness in this world too!"

" You know what I have already done and ventured! Do you imagine that I will hesitate at another crime to reach the goal for which I have struggled. You little idiot! with your greed turned into love spasms. Leave me in doubt to-day, allow me to doubt in the future, and your egotistic abortion of a doctor shall suffer for it. I have spared him so far on your account—it was part of the agreement—and I kept it despite the trouble and anxiety it has caused me. Forget your oath, and I swear that his life shall be a part payment for the treachery. You know me!"

There was a silence of a few minutes, broken at last by the woman's voice, which had lost its musical sweetness, and was now forced and harsh.

"Order! What am I to do?"

"Keep on as you have been doing. In a few days you are free. I will personally see to your future happiness; or you are free to go where you will. It is now necessary that she should be ruined for the safety of both. If necessary, next time tap her on the head! I should prefer her to face her degradation in full consciousness, but if you fear 'spies', mutilate her—curse her!—do any thing but kill her. That will come later, in the form of a rope!"

"I can not do that!"

"Keep in your place, then; preserve your old attitude, and when I have ended the business here, I will come to your help and do what you fear to do."

"It is impossible."

"Nothing is impossible to me and my hatred, as you know! I will venture in their midst, and escape from it unharmed, after I have paid my devotions to your lady! Curse her, and trebly curse her! You stare. Doubt as much as you like, only heed and obey me. Stay where you are, her present state will last until I am ready for her. Play the saint, the fiend or the angel, any thing but the traitor, and I am content."

"I can not help myself."

"I am glad you have reached that wise conclusion. Now let me show your idiocy out! I have already wasted the time I can not spare, and I must bury him to-day. Come! end your snivel until you are safe at home."

At this point Miss Churchill hastily withdrew, and hid herself in the black shadows of the vault below. The conversation continued some time longer in the room above; but she heard only a confused sound, instead of words. The murmur died away; and there was the echo of footsteps descending the stone stairs. Two figures entered the vault, crossed and passed into the dark tunnel on the other side.

When they had disappeared, Miss Churchill emerged from her retreat, noiselessly ascended the steps and entered the room above. She glanced at the door and discovered it was of massive stone, like the walls of the room itself. A tall, curiously-shaped room, with a single narrow window in the thick wall; built in an angle of the house, with stone ceiling, stone walls and stone floor; empty, save for a small bench just beneath the window. A narrow, winding stone stairway crossed it at its center; this Miss Churchill ascended, and found herself in another room similar to the one below, but of double its height, and with a ceiling converging on all sides to a central point. The stairway abruptly ceased in this room; but a heavy stone door was on the side opposite the window. A huge bolt was in this door; but it was drawn back, and pulling on the ring which served in place of a handle, Miss Churchill opened it; passed through, while the door slowly swung to and closed with a metallic "*click*". She was now in a hallway of what was once the inhabited part of the house;

she had entered at its center, and it ran in curving line from north to south. Before venturing further, she turned to look at the door ; but though she had just passed through she could not discover it. Its surface was covered with the same paper that lined the hall walls, and its lines of junction were undiscovered by her sharp eyes or practiced fingers.

Fearing discovery, she glided onward, and had hardly hidden herself behind the tapestry that was half drawn back from before the entrance to a dark room, when the door again opened, and an old, gray-haired man appeared in the hallway. He went in the direction opposite that she had taken, and descended a broad flight of stairs at the other side of the hall, passing a window that extended from roof to floor of the hall, and through which the light streamed on his sedate figure and venerable face. His footsteps still sounded, descending lower and lower the flights of uncarpeted stairs.

Miss Churchill now left her place of concealment, crossed the hall, and glanced out the high, narrow window. Gazing downward, the land that connected the house with the village was in the line of her vision ; and, after a brief interval, she saw a sober, sedate figure cross this piece of land and disappear. She now descended the stairs, anxious to get safely out of the trap into which she had knowingly entered. Flight after flight she descended, meeting with no one, and caring to meet with no one.

She reached the hallway of the lowest story, and

the door of exit was before her ; but she could not resist glancing in the open doorway into the large somber room which was fitted up as a library.

A desk littered with papers was temptingly near the door. She approached it, selected one of the papers—the detective's memoranda of the case—and placed it in her pocket. She then seized a sheet of blank paper, and, with a smile on her lips, wrote the words : " *To the most vigilant* of detectives, from his admirer, Miss O. G."

She now opened the front door, tripped to the veranda only to face a local police-officer, who stared at her in ludicrous amazement.

" Who are you, ma'am ? " he asked, fiercely, conquering his fear. She gracefully handed him the order that the detective had written at the doctor's request.

The policeman received it superciliously, and read : " *Please treat the bearer of this with the utmost courtesy, and give the same liberty of action as if you were dealing with the undersigned.—J. Sharpe, Detective.*"

The policeman handed it back to the woman with a shrug of the shoulders, which he converted into an : " Excuse me, ma'am, I didn't know ! "

" I excuse and thank you."

She smiled, opened her umbrella and passed out into the storm.

CHAPTER XIII.

CUNNING MATCHES CUNNING.

WHEN Miss Churchill returned to Woodbine Villa she retired first to her room to change her rain-soaked garments ; then descended to the invalid's room. At her appearance, the doctor, who was playing the part of nurse, cast aside his book, and advanced to meet her with a smiling face.

"She sleeps quietly, doctor," she said, glancing critically toward the pale yet tranquil face on the pillow.

"More quietly than I hoped. Are you satisfied with the results of your journey?"

"They have been fairly satisfactory. I have paid a visit to Ralph Price, and by threats and cunning and promises discovered that he has never seen Miss Gower in his life. What he said to the detective he has been taught to say, and it's my belief his teacher was Max Newton."

"This conclusion is in entire harmony with my scientific deductions," said the doctor, approvingly.

"I always had the greatest respect for science, but I have not time now to indulge in its praises. It is my desire that Miss Percy return to her old position near the patient. You will please tell her that the volatile Miss Churchill has grown tired of playing the part of nurse and prefers to sleep in her own room."

" But—" began the astonished doctor.

" Miss Percy is reinstated here as maid," insisted the other, " and you are to tell her, in a diplomatic way, of course, that *professionally* you are deeply interested in the recovery of your patient. You will detain Miss Percy here for a couple of hours this evening, as I intend to search her room."

" Oh ! I begin to understand you ! Is there any thing else ? "

" One more item, doctor. Before I went away this morning, I scribbled a note to Captain Travers. Can you tell me if he received it ? "

" All my information is contained in the statement that he left the house in a very hurried manner, without informing me of his intentions or destination. He took a hand-satchel with him, and in parting with me told me he did not know when he should return."

" He has then received my note," said Miss Churchill, sinking into an arm-chair with a sigh of relief. " Your watch is over for the present, doctor. Perhaps, however, it may be well to inform Miss Percy that I have been deposed. Tell her that in your indignation you have brought me to a sense of my duty. It will cause her to regard you more favorably."

" But I do not wish her regards ! " growled the doctor, irritably.

" It will help us—and she is pretty ! "

The doctor gazed suspiciously at his friend to detect the incipient symptoms of mockery or satire, but the sphinx-face defied his scrutiny, and he left the room the victim of suppressed irritation.

Miss Churchill solaced her loneliness by reading the manuscript that she had stolen from the library in the old house.   It was dull reading for a woman, as it consisted of nothing but detached names, and long columns of figures.   Yet it absorbed all her attention, and the rustle of Miss Percy's dress startled her as if she had heard the report of a cannon.   She had been engaged a long hour in her study of the manuscript, and even then it had not revealed its secret.

There was no weariness in Miss Percy's face ; a natural bloom was on her cheeks ; her eyes were bright, although they were unusually serious ; but that added to, rather than detracted from, her dainty beauty.

" Can I serve you with any refreshments, Miss Churchill ? " she asked, seriously hospitable. " Dinner is still an hour away ! "

" I ain't hungry, Miss Percy, but I'm glad you've got over your airs.   I'm good-natured when I see people in their places, but I never could stand seeing servants acting like their mistresses."

" Is it not equally bad for the mistress to assume

the part of the servant ? " asked Miss Percy, with a smile.

" It is very tiresome, at least ; and I've no objection for you to take that labor off my shoulders. Though how even you can pass your life at beck and call of another I can't understand. Where were you born ? " she asked, indulging in the liberty which one woman boldly assumes toward the other when she is higher in the social scale.

" I was born in Manchester, England. My father was a manufacturer of cotton ; rich and good, and my real name is Perceval and *not* Percy."

The explanation was given with a quiet unaffectedness that favorably impressed the suspicious Miss Churchill.

" Rich ? And you in service ? "

" His second wife was a widow with five children of her own. She did not love me, or I her. I was scratched from the will. When my father died, I ran away from home to this country, trusting for protection to an uncle, who closed his door in my face. *He* was rich, too, but he left me to starvation, or worse, without a care ! "

" What is your uncle's business ? "

" I suppose *you* would call him a servant. He *was* major domo, half servant, half friend. Perhaps he is master himself now, who knows ? "

" Are you friendly with him ? "

" As friendly as you would be with a man who held a pistol to your head ! He needs me ! But there is the first bell for dinner ringing ! "

Miss Churchill hastily retired, and Miss Percy sank into an arm-chair, and, in imagination, filled the fingers of her pretty but unadorned hands with a number of rings. But she was not in an amiable mood ; having passed through the bitter experience that had taught her to suspect everybody else, she had reached a less satisfying stage of thought, and began to suspect herself. With strange perversity, she thought less of the dangers of the present, than of the hopes of the future.

She was sad and discouraged, although the road to fortune and social position was open before her. Glancing backward, it seemed to her that the labor was hardly worth the pains. She was troubled with hesitations and doubts. It was a gloomy life, after all ; and even if she succeeded, there was very little to live for. There are worse things in the world than starvation ; and diamond rings, in themselves, are not necessarily nobler ornaments than iron rings. There was less difficulty in saving herself than in respecting herself ! The pendulum of her thoughts swung with monotonous regularity between Max Newton and Doctor Dubois. The former had her hate and the latter her contempt ; yet her safety depended on the one, and her happiness or misery on the other, and the choice was very difficult to make.

" Better stake all to win all, than lead this wretched life ! " was her thought. " If I can hang him before he kills me, I shall be lucky ! He forced me to enter the path, and let him take the con-

sequences. A poor price for years of honesty,
suffering, and misery," she thought with dismal
regret. " In a moment I have become every thing
I feared to be, and suffered starvation that I might
not be! But they are all the same ! " she thought,
yielding to the solace of sweeping generalization ;
" all the same, only I still detest what they are
taught to worship as a necessary evil. A ball-
room is worse," she thought, with a frown on her
face. "Only the difference is, that I am struggling
for life, and they to show their shamelessness. My
one only honest pride," she thought, her regret
merged into a painful humiliation. " Even death
to that ! " she thought, with her eyes turned
moodily toward the bed. " I will become deadened
to it, like to all the rest, and the sooner the better !
The devil has left that to me as an anticipation of
the future ! The doctor would call it a mania," she
thought, her face hardening into sternness. " An
anomaly ! Shame in a shameless one ! Prudery in
a poisoner ! " This with another glance at the bed.
" *He*, too, would let me starve, if it were not for my
pretty shoulders and my boldness. The doctor !
the doctor ! I am selling myself like a decent
woman, without a decent woman's love of the
transaction ! "

She again glanced down at her white, dimpled
hands, and her eyes wandered from her fingers to
her wrists.

" Many have sold their souls for less," she
thought, removing the plain gold bangle from her

wrist with a shudder. "And I will become deadened to it! deadened to it! The doctor! the doctor! What is left me to love but gold and dress! They blast me with the evil in their eyes that their tongues dare not speak! Fools they, and fool I; only I will use them to exalt myself!"

Miss Percy continued her meditations; but she no longer thought of the one humiliation that she submitted to, yet which caused her the sharpest agony—the insult to her maidenly modesty! She defied it; would perhaps defy it again and again, but it was there, and every act of defiance was followed by a flood of bitter tears! An anomaly in such a being? But in the muddiest pools there is some distorted reflection of heaven; in every mire-stained, wind-tossed leaf some suggestion of a dead summer of which it was a part. An anomaly! The doctor! the doctor!

But Miss Percy resolutely subdued her pain, and again directed her attention to the real danger that menaced her. Here she could summon her energy and her pride; her scorn and her cynicism; and here work on more congenial subjects.

The early twilight settled heavily around her, and blotted her out of sight. From the drawing-room below came the faint sounds of music. Miss Churchill was evidently amusing her host and her host's friends with songs. It was a part of the farce!

Miss Percy rose, lighted the gas, and then gazed at herself in the mirror.

" *He* is dangerous ! " she said mockingly, " and I do not look badly ! Perhaps he will ask me to copy another lying report. The poor, silly man ! "

She turned from the glass to bathe the face of the sleeping woman ; adjust the disheveled hair, and smooth down the pillows. This labor done, she stood for a moment by the bedside, contemplating her work.

" I shall never indulge in opium. She was pretty before she took it ; but in a few days she has grown ten years older."

The unconscious woman feebly murmured in her sleep.

" She is dreaming of the gallant captain ! If I hated her, I should rejoice at her recovery ; if she were my sister and I loved her, I would let her die. And she has been kind to me ! I might cry, if I had time to think of it ! "

She gently lifted the heavy arms and arranged them in a more comfortable position, and then turned away from the bed.

She welcomed the doctor, who now entered, with a joyous little laugh.

" I am anxious to see the condition of my patient when she wakes. I hope it will be favorable, for I have staked my reputation on her complete recovery."

" Then she *must* and *shall* get well ! " exclaimed the young woman determinedly. " Only you must not allow Miss Churchill to interfere with me again ! "

" I think I have convinced her rustic mind that

good manners require her to attend to her own business ! "

Miss Percy became silently thoughtful for a moment, then said, with a certain anxiety :

" You are very much interested in Miss Gower, and she is very pretty ! "

" You foolish child ! A doctor is not a man ! If Miss Gower were the most hideous of women, my interest in her would be exactly the same. After I have cured her, I am indifferent—I never was fond of her ! But I am vain of my skill, my dear, and rather than have it fail here, I would submit to almost any other humiliation ! "

The cloud vanished from Miss Percy's face.

" Your skill *will* conquer ; I'm sure of it ! " she said gayly ; "and since you are so *very* much interested, I would give my life rather than you should fail ! "

CHAPTER XIV.

WHILE the doctor is employed in entertaining Miss Percy, Miss Churchill is employed in examining Miss Percy's room. She goes about her work in a calm, systematic manner, neglecting nothing, forgetting nothing. She did not expect to find much of a compromising nature, for, although Miss Percy was foolish, it was not probable that she would keep possession of any thing that would place a rope around her neck. Nevertheless, the experienced Miss Churchill thought it very probable that articles or manuscript that compromised her might be found.

Her expectation might be interpreted in these words :

" The woman shares in the crime, but, in addition to the danger that menaces all, there is an individual danger as well. Criminals are suspicious of each other, and to prevent an anticipated treachery, they will keep something which, in case of danger, they can hold as a Damocles' sword over their faint-hearted companions. Now, it is very probable that Miss Percy has held back something that she may use against the old man who plays the part of tyrannical master to her. She fears him and wishes to escape from him, and if he has written to her any thing of a compromising nature, I shall find it here!"

Miss Churchill proceeded to submit this theory to the strain of facts. A large trunk stood in the corner of the room, and was the first object that naturally attracted Miss Churchill's attention. It was an ordinary canvas covered trunk, but of more than ordinary strength; and it was fastened by a large, complicated-looking steel lock. It might have resisted a bungler's attempt at opening it; but it readily yielded to the slender twisted instrument that Miss Churchill applied to it. Having opened the lock and unfastened the strap, she lifted the lid. It was, apparently, filled with dresses, and other articles of woman's attire. These Miss Churchill carefully removed, and was unrewarded for her pains; for she reached the bottom of the trunk without discovering any thing that even faintly supported her theory. She glanced at the empty trunk, and then, taking a tape measure from her pocket, measured it from the outside and then from the inside. She was not in the least surprised that the contrasted measurements indicated a false bottom.

Kneeling before the trunk, she carefully examined it, and solved the secret. She pressed against a small projection to her right on the side of the trunk, and the false bottom was lifted several inches by concealed springs. She raised it still further, and discovered, as she expected to discover, several small bundles of letters ; each package carefully tied in a ribbon. A few loose papers, one or two small books, and a lock of hair, completed the list of the contents of this hiding-place. She glanced at the front pages of the books, and then returned them to their place. One was a small volume of fairy tales, and bore on one of its fly-leaves the words : " To May Perceval, from her affectionate father. Manchester, 18—" Another bulkier volume was a manual on Comparative Physiology and Zoology, and bore as inscription : " To Miss Percy, from her friend, A. Dubois, M.D. Cypressville. August 30, 18——" There was a pamphlet with the title of " How to live on sixpence a day ! " There was no dedication ; but across the title was written, in a woman's hand. " How shall we live without a sixpence ? "

Miss Churchill was not interested in this question. She carried the letters to a table, seated herself before it, and carefully examined her prizes.

One package contained a number of letters dated years back ; letters addressed by a loving father and mother to their child. Their only interest to Miss Churchill was, that as far as they went, they verified the account Miss Percy had given of herself.

Another small package contained letters that were also of a domestic nature. They ranged through several years, and were mostly stern, cruel answers to some one who had requested something.

Miss Churchill read these letters carefully, and made mental notes of several significant paragraphs. One letter she boldly appropriated, after reading it through with strong symptoms of disgust and horror. This bundle more than vindicated another portion of Miss Percy's account of herself.

Here is a paragraph from a letter with a date that indicated it was nearly two years old :

" Why repeat and repeat that you are starving ? Starve, and don't bother me about it ! I made you an offer once, and you refused it. As you prize what you call your 'innocence' so much, cling to it and starve ! If you want my assistance, you can only get it by accepting the conditions I impose. Your ideas are too lofty. When they come lower down, write to me ; but not till then ! "

The letters all indicated harsh, unrelenting cruelty on one side ; pitiful pleadings on the other.

Miss Churchill tied up this bundle, minus one letter, and thrust it from her with disgust.

Among the remaining letters there was one that particularly interested her ; it was addressed to Miss Gower, and had, probably, been stolen from her with other similar matter by the treacherous maid. The letter was written in July of the previous year, " *On board the steam yacht Oriana,*" and was to the following effect :

" MY DEAR SISTER : Your persistent obstinacy pains me to the heart ! This is the twelfth letter I have written to you and received no answer. If I am willing to forget the past, why will you show so much unwillingness? The troubles you have brought on yourself are of your own making. Years ago I bowed down in adoration, and I feel the same unquenchable passion for you now! Had you heeded me, I would have devoted my life to making you happy. But you had provincial ideas then, and you have them now. I have tried to forget you, but you remain to me what you always were. My poor Oriana! If you only had my experience, you would discover how foolish and isolated you are in your prejudices. I intend, shortly, to go away on a long pleasure excursion. Come and share it with me, and if, after the experiment, you still retain your old ideas, you can return to the life you so much prize. If you consent, you may persuade me to any thing, even to believe in your sermons; if you do not, I shall continue in my old way, only the vise will squeeze harder. I love you, and I am determined to have my way; your obstinacy only increases my ardor. What I can not gain you will lose. Remember your past experience, and learn from it the depth of my passion and of my determination. If you do not answer this, you will feel the energy of the wretched man whose love you have so long scorned. Forgive and forget, as I do, and come to the loving arms of your slave and worshipper,

"HUGO."

This was the only letter that seemed even remotely related to the murdered man.

" She has surrendered the others—if others there
were—to her taskmaster," was Miss Churchill's mental comment. " Her taskmaster and *his* devoted
friend ! "

She took the liberty of appropriating this letter,
also, and carefully deposited it in her pocket.

Among the loose letters was the following, without address or date :

" Come to me immediately, and you shall not
starve, if you have courage and firmness. You
are welcome to your virtuous determinations, but if
you come to me and obey my instructions to the
letter, you will be the better off by many hundreds
of dollars, and I will promise you my unfailing protection. Come, then, show your spirit and escape
starvation and the gutter ! I will pay
your wretched debts and be a liberal uncle to
you."

This was the last prize that Miss Churchill won
and deposited in her capacious pocket. She returned the letters to their hiding-place, closed the
concealing top, carefully restored the dresses and
other articles to their places in the trunk, shut
down the lid, and with the slender, twisted little
instrument locked it.

She now continued her examination of the
room ; but after the most thorough search discovered nothing that repaid her for the trouble,
except one mysterious object which was found in
the desk near the window. This object was a
small rectangular piece of Bristol board with a line

of figures and a line of words. The upper quarter
is reproduced as a specimen :

    1. Here.
1—2. Peace.
2—1. Trouble.
2—2. Danger.
2—3. Must see you.
3—2. Will meet you.
2—4. Spies.
4—2. You are watched.

" *Count five between each number. Once every
night.*"

It was suggestive of a child's game or something
else. Miss Churchill copied it in her note-book
and returned it to its place in the desk. A quaint
old bull's-eye lantern was standing on the mantle,
claiming admiration among other curious ornaments.
Its owner would have truly asserted that it was over
two hundred years old, but a piece of very modern
wax-candle was contained within it, indicating that
its practical utility was still unimpaired.

The results of the examination were not disap-
pointing ; they fully supported Miss Churchill's
theory, even to the extent of demonstrating the
foolishness of my lady's maid, who had, evidently,
never expected that her room would be searched ;
or suspicion attach to her as being one of the
instruments in the great crime. Her simplicity
was deserving of contempt, and also of pity ! She
was only an amateur criminal after all ; compelled

to enter the path of crime, not from inclination,
but from necessity. Properly managed, she might
prove of great assistance in the further work of
examination, as Miss Churchill argued; even to
the extent of running her own vain head in the
noose, if such a result could not be avoided!

Miss Churchill cast one last glance around the
neat, tasty little room, and then retired to enjoy a
breath of fresh air in the cupola.

She had no difficulty in reaching it. It was a
fair-sized room, carpeted and furnished, and heavy
with the rich perfume of the flowers that rested on
brackets between the windows. An octagonal
room, perched high above the tree tops, and thus,
from its numerous windows, presenting charming
views of the surrounding country.

Unfortunately, the night was dark, and Miss
Churchill had no opportunity for indulging her
artistic tastes. But, at least, she could satisfy her
curiosity by gazing in the direction of the house
in which the murder was committed. Nothing was
visible; but an universal blackness. This disappointment did not disturb Miss Churchill, even
though she had assisted her eyes with a powerful
field-glass. She quietly seated herself in a rustic
chair, and watched with an obstinate patience.

The rain had ceased; but the sky was still
cloudy. The wind had increased to a gale, and its
icy breath was converting the moisture on the
windows into incipient frost. Under a clearer sky,
the orchards might have suffered; but, at least,

winter was giving its warning of a very early approach this year.

Miss Churchill amused her leisure by thinking of trivial subjects ; but with her face turned always in one direction. A flash of light, high up, in the distance, startled her ! One flash, and then darkness. She had brought the old bull's-eye lantern in the cupola, and she now lighted the candle in it and waved it once near the window, and then lowered it. There was an answering flash, and thus another one of her surmises was proved ; an occupant of Woodbine Villa could communicate by signals with an occupant of the old house. Again the light flashed in the distance : one, two ; then a pause, then one ! This signified " TROUBLE ", according to the strange code of signals she had discovered. With admirable presence of mind she flashed the signals indicating " PEACE ". Again the light appeared, *one, two—one ! two !—one—two !* A long pause. Then *one, two, three—one, two, three;* and darkness. Consulting the code, she discovered that she had been thus warned : *Prepare for flight —The tree !*

Telegraphy in its infancy ; but none the less effectual on that account !

She waited for further information ; but the signaling was seemingly over for the night. Detailed information was, probably, concealed in the tree, whose secret she had already solved. With characteristic energy, she determined to finish her night's work by paying a visit to the robin's-nest letter box. It might contain important matter which would be lost if she waited till the next day, as her visit might be anticipated by the foolish lady's maid.

Thus far she had been unexpectedly successful, and she was almost at the heart of the mystery.

She retired to her room to dress herself in warmer attire. For this purpose she opened her trunk, which had only arrived in the morning, and which she had not had time to unpack. It had been especially made on a plan of her own, and the lock was so ingeniously constructed that she would have defied the most expert burglar to pick it, or open the trunk at all without mutilating it. Thinking of the trunk she had recently examined, she smiled as she busied herself with the lock of her own.

To change her attire was the work of a few minutes ; and in less time, she had cautiously made her exit from the house, and was sturdily battling with the wind out in the open air. But time was precious ; she had to give the doctor notice that her work was ended, and he at liberty to leave the presence of the fascinating Miss Percy ; and she had, also, to prepare for the labors of the morrow. The icy wind could not deter her ; let it shriek ever so much in the branches overhead ; she was used to this species of work. A September night, with the chilled breath issuing from her lips like smoke ! But it was fortunate ; for it only incited her to walk the quicker. Yes ; to her left was the old

house rising grim and black ; no lights in its window, and a deep fog rising about its base. Were the
criminals as foolish as are most criminals, or was
she unusually clever ? There was the tree just in
front of her ; she could have selected it out of
thousands ; with its rough moss-grown trunk and its
huge overhanging branches, tossing and writhing
under the tortures of the wind ! The robin's-nest
was in the fork formed by two branches ; and to
reach it, one had to stand on tip-toe, and assist
one's self by clinging to one of the down-hanging
boughs. There was no need to tell Miss Churchill
this ; she grasped the branch with her left
hand, raised herself on tip-toe, and reached out
toward the nest, but did not touch it ; for she
received a heavy blow from some weapon that
struck her on the side of the head and then glanced
off to her shoulder ! She fell to the ground without
uttering a sound, and a heavy branch of the tree
fell with her. For a moment she was stunned ;
had she received the blow fairly on the top of her
head she would have been killed ! She lay passive
in the wet grass for a time, and then with an
effort rose to her feet, the world swimming around
her, and the pain in her shoulder more unbearable
than the pain in her head. The wind had evidently partially twisted off from the parent tree
the overhanging branch, and the additional weight
had brought it down on her head ! That was the
probable explanation of the humiliating accident.
But the brave Miss Churchill would not acknowl-

edge defeat. She bit her lips to repress her groans, and again stretched out her arm toward the robin's-nest. With an effort she reached it, but the expected letter was not in it ! In her eagerness she had come too soon, and in her dazed condition she forgot to examine the strange weapon that had struck her.

Her head was tied up in a handkerchief when she entered the room to bid the doctor good evening ; but later in the night she submitted herself to his care, and explained to him the cause of her accident. He congratulated her on her wonderful escape.

" Had the blow been direct, Miss Churchill, it is probable it would have fractured the base of your skull ! You will recover long before our patient ! "

" You are disappointed ? " she asked, resolutely interesting herself in the fate of another, while the doctor was dressing her own wounds.

"She waked up conscious enough ; but what with her tears, shrieks and pleadings, the other condition was less dangerous. If the business is not cleared up in a few days, I fear the result. She is in some way mixed up with it, and unless we can positively reassure her, she will worry herself into a brain-fever. To tell you the truth, I am discouraged."

" Repeat that in two days from now, doctor, and I will answer, that you are hard to please ! You have eased my pains, and in gratitude I will

ease your anxieties ; and the foolish Miss Percy
shall unconsciously help me to do so."

At that moment the foolish Miss Percy was in
her own room gazing smilingly down on her
trunk.

" She will question me to-morrow, and I must
answer—as much as I dare ! It is safe on that side
—to-morrow I will make it safe on the other ! And
the doctor is a bore after all ! What a pity it is
that the good old times are gone when a lover
could be changed into a shower of gold ! And I
am to pass the night in my lady's room ; they are
so sure of me that they cease to fear me. Heigh-
ho ! I wonder how long it will be before I can
sleep in a bed of my own ! I wish I could pitch
away the hand he squeezed ! Fortunately I can
sleep on a lounge as well as in a bed, and if he
must be summoned he will not surprise me in a
hideous night-gown ! "

Another morning dawned, announcing a day that
was to be filled with surprises. Miss Percy rose
before the sun, bright and refreshed ; Miss
Churchill rose with the sun, with an acute headache and a painful shoulder, but also with undi-
minished energy. She entered the patient's room
while the doctor was still peacefully snoring in his
bed, and displayed an unwonted friendliness
toward Miss Percy, which that young lady appreciated.

" I almost envy you, Miss Percy. Here I have
been sleeping on a comfortable bed and wake up

looking a fright, while you sleep on a sofa and get up as bright as the sun."

" I'm used to sleeping anywhere. I have slept on an uncarpeted floor and very comfortably too ! "

" While your uncle enjoyed himself at his ease, the brute. Did you know his master ? "

" My sweet uncle wished to force an acquaintance-ship on me, but I objected, and that angered him."

" Why did you object? was not the master a gentleman ? "

" A hypocrite and a fiend, Miss Churchill. Had I been less obstinate, I might at the present moment have owned a little milliner's store in this village, instead of being a lady's-maid."

" Where is he now ? "

" My uncle could tell you better than I ! " said Miss Percy with a smile.

" What is his name ? "

" Pardon me if I like my life too well to utter it."

" You are not frank with me," said Miss Churchill, careless now of disguise. " Suppose I could name your uncle and his master. Suppose I am bold enough to venture into Max Newton's presence, and ask him what he has done with his master Hugo Addison ? "

Miss Churchill enjoyed her triumph ; the sur-prise and dismay of the maid flattered her profes-sional vanity.

" You are a witch ! "

" And you a coward to allow your uncle to

endanger your young life. I will be your friend, if
you will meet me half way. Think over it, and when
I see you again, your profit or disadvantage depends
on the words you then speak to me ! "

There was a sternness in Miss Churchill's voice,
and unusual dignity in her manners, as she swept
from the room.

Miss Percy's gravity followed the woman ; she
laughed gayly.

" She is walking into *my* trap, instead of me walking into hers. It is sometimes good to be thought
a fool ! "

She blithely continued her labors of dusting and
arranging the furniture, glancing now and then
toward the door ; and now and then toward the
looking-glass ; a laughing type of amiable malice.
Miss Churchill's condescension had conquered even
her anxieties, and, with her destiny trembling in the
balance, she recklessly surrendered herself to the
enjoyment of the minute ; her suppressed mirth
accumulating until she dissipated it in a burst of
of light, ringing, musical laughter.

When the doctor came to pay his morning visit to
the room, her face had assumed its seriousness ; but
bright points of mischief were still dancing in her
eyes. A servant followed the doctor, carrying
a salver on which was food for the sick
woman.

With an anxious face, the doctor gently roused the
sleeper, who started into a sitting position at his
slight touch, and stared wildly around her. Miss

Percy now waved him aside, and took his place near her mistress.

"You must have had frightful dreams last night, Miss Gower. And you made me so nervous that I sat up with you, and now have called the doctor to my aid!"

The calm, smiling face of the maid reassured the mistress; she sighed, but the wild expression faded from her eyes.

"Have I been here long?"

"Only since I put you into bed last night. I think you must have caught cold playing croquet yesterday morning."

"Is *he* here?"

With fine instinct, the maid divined the mistress's thoughts, and, to the doctor's admiration, soothed them.

"It was a false rumor. It was not his yacht at all; and it is now supposed that the first rumor was correct, and that it was lost in the waves."

The mistress sighed heavily, and sank back on the pillow, relieved in heart and mind, and too weary to analyze the comforting statement.

"It was a strange dream!"

"A bad night-mare! But you must take a little nourishment, and then try and sleep again; for Captain Travers is anxious to have his revenge."

The mistress flushed at the name, quietly accepted nourishment from the hands of the maid, and then, like a tired child, fell into a peaceful sleep, with a spoonful of untasted food at her lips.

The doctor's admiration was unbounded.

"It was a stroke of genius!" he exclaimed, enthusiastically, "the one only remedy applied at the one proper instant of time."

"I am working for my new position!" she said, demurely.

"And you shall have it, I pledge you my word. But you must first have full confidence in me and I in you."

"Must we exchange references, sir?"

"Rather we must be frank. I am your friend. Tell me, then, all you know."

"I know I am very wretched and of a very jealous nature. I am a foolish woman; I was born independent, and I have the ugly trick of imagining that by birth and education I am the equal of any one. There are certain rumors in the village which connect my name with one whom the world honors; my anger was stilled in remembering that my reputation was blasted by a great genius whom I—I—really cared for! For the first time in my life I saw my ideal of a hero realized in him—and—and I was foolishly happy," she said, with a deep flush, that extended even to her pretty ears.

Barring that he felt that the colored pattern on his dressing gown did not match his complexion, and that a hero lost some of his dignity in slippers, the doctor received the statement in calm satisfaction.

"You are a foolish, impetuous child!" he said, good naturedly. "But I like your frankness."

"Foolish to the extent of becoming insanely

jealous ; of drugging the woman whom I stupidly regarded as my rival."

Ah ! how complex is woman's nature. Here was a young creature, a decidedly pretty young woman, who had allowed herself to commit a crime out of her love for a man of his sedate age. Not that he was old ! At fifty a man is in the prime of vigorous life ! Age was not in the question. But it *was* surprising that a young creature of her gayety should fall in love with a person of his gravity of character. For once Mr. Morris was right !

"As I understand you, my child, your evil treatment of your mistress was due to jealousy, and nothing else ?"

" To jealousy alone. I thought the opium would make her look ugly, and that my hero——"

The reappearance of Miss Churchill interrupted what promised to be a very intimate conversation, and gave the abashed maid an opportunity to retire. But before leaving the room, she asked :

" Could I in safety leave my mistress for a couple of hours ?"

"I shall be here for that length of time," said the doctor, after receiving an approving nod from the new-comer.

"And please do not forget what I have said," added Miss Churchill. " To-day you must decide whether I am to be your friend or enemy."

" I am not likely to forget. My absence is connected with the subject about which you intend to speak. Let her follow me !" thought Miss Percy, as she ascended to her room. " She will only rub her nose against a rock this time. If *I* had prepared the tree-branch she wouldn't have escaped with a scratch. But men are born fools ! "

" She is going to see the man Newton," said Miss Churchill to the doctor. "*He* is the murderer, and she is trying to escape from his claws. We have evidence to show that he is deeply interested in the crime ; but none to prove that he was directly concerned in it. While free, he may compromise himself by some hasty act ; in jail, we are hopeless."

" But if Miss Percy——"

" She can tell us nothing bearing on this one vital point. The man is too cunning to trust the secret, even with her. He has managed to blind the very detective who is always beside him. He is a criminal of brains, and they are the worst of all ! "

" Yet you made a very definite promise, and seemed to have great hope."

" I have it still ; but the more I think over the subject, the more perplexed I grow. If I could only discover the reason of the man's hatred to Miss Gower ; or if I could find the man Draper, I should solve the one doubt that confuses me. I wrote some instructions for the use of Captain Travers, and I sent him to the city ; partly to help us, and partly to keep him in ignorance of the danger hovering over his friend."

" Have you heard from him ? "

"One of his directions was to make inquiries concerning the murdered man's yacht, the *Oriana*. He was to visit the dockyard in which it was repaired, and also find out where it is now. I have just received his telegram on this subject. Here it is." Miss Churchill read from the paper in her hand : "'Yacht nowhere. Not been seen since repaired. Not in harbor. Will write.' That is the captain's message."

"Might I ask why you are interested in the yacht?"

"I am not accustomed to anticipate my actions by describing them ; but for once I will break through my custom. From the start, I have believed Max Newton to be the murderer !"

"Science irrefragably pointed to the same conclusion," said the doctor, pompously.

Miss Churchill continued, without heeding the interruption :

"Max Newton is the murderer ! Why then should Mr. Draper so mysteriously disappear ? He has no reason of his own ; no reason to desert the woman with whom he has been intimate ; whether innocently or guiltily, I can not say ! But if we suppose he possessed some knowledge, the publication of which would compromise Max Newton, we have an explanation. The murderer removed him from his path, either by committing another blood-crime, or by secreting his victim. Reaching this point, my mind naturally reverted to the yacht, and to find it was a part of the captain's instructions. If it were readily found, I was willing to dismiss it from my mind; as it was not readily found, I have sent telegrams to the city ordering skilled agents to discover its whereabouts."

" Your argument is weighty, and I am surprised that I did not think of it," said the doctor, thoughtfully.

" As to the will business that so troubles Detective Sharpe, it is easily solved. As the confidant of his master, Max Newton knew that a fresh will, disinheriting Miss Gower, was to be signed. In his inexplicable hatred of our patient, he killed his master at the very moment when the circumstantial evidence would tell against Miss Gower ! "

" But why was the crime committed at all ? "

" I will give you the sum of my information. Master and man were both creatures of strong passions; despite his local reputation, Mr. Addison was a strong sensualist—I have read one of his letters, and it supports what I have elsewhere learned ; the servant gained power over him by consenting to be his vile agent ; even attempting to lure his own niece into sin. Master and man quarreled, as was inevitable under the circumstances. And, further, the servant is avaricious ; the desire to sell his own niece proves this. They quarrel ; the master is anxious to cast off the servant, who has become a burden on him ; he wants to make his selections himself ; he refuses to pay his servant his price ; these reasons are amply sufficient to account for the murder, especially when

we remember the ten thousand dollars, which we
know, and the many thousand dollars of which we
do not know, that fell into the murderer's hands.
The master was a careless spendthrift, caring only
for his pleasures; the servant had passed that
stage, and cared only for his self-interest. Money
was the principal cause of the murder, whatever
may have been the secondary causes; and Max
Newton is the only one that profited by it ! To-
day I intend to devote to studying and investigating
this aspect of the subject."

"Can I be of any help?"

"Yes; you would oblige me if you would call
on Detective Sharpe and quietly discover if he has
blundered on any truths. I expected to see him
in triumph here before sunrise with an order of
arrest. His absence demonstrates that he is losing
his faith in his theory. I shall pay my first visit to
Mr. Terms; you had better wait the return of the
foolish maid."

"You do not think she is guilty?" asked the
doctor, with an anxiety that was stronger than the
attempt made to conceal it.

" I think we are acquainted with the worst crime
of that wretched young woman ; and if she is not
compliant to my wishes sne shall suffer for it ! She
shall find that an attempt at poison is not a slight
thing !"

The doctor saw, in a flash, the young lady on the
witness stand explaining the reason for her actions,
and, in her simplicity, relating the scandals that he

had unwittingly brought upon her. He saw his name gracing the head-lines of all the morning papers, and anticipated the editorials, wherein would be discussed how "a distinguished citizen, a man of universal reputation in his profession, deliberately forgot his noble calling ; tampered with the affections of a young maiden, blasted her character, and then, in his Don Juan indifference, goaded her into crime !" He had been seen with his arm around her waist ; she had been seen in his bed-room. The day was cold, but the doctor mopped the perspiration from his forehead with his handkerchief and concealed his face at the same time.

"I think, Miss Churchill, that the young lady will tell all she knows."

"A taste of jail will cure her obstinacy ! She is too dainty to suffer that disgrace long."

"She is impetuous, Miss Churchill, but not chronically bad. In such cases, a little toleration is the wisest course."

"But an attempt at poison, doctor ! "

"Hardly that. She was, perhaps, ordered by her cruel taskmaster to keep his victim unconscious, so that she could not interfere with his plans !" said the doctor, with a flash of inspiration.

"It is very probable," answered Miss Churchill, thoughtfully.

"It is *certain !* " retorted the doctor, persuasively. "I have thought the matter over, but until now have not ventured to interrupt your investigations

with my conclusions. You will find, Miss Churchill,
that science is right here as elsewhere, and that
from Miss Gower's own lips you will hear the
justification of my deduction. And we shall
speedily know," he added, turning to the bed
where the sleeper was smiling in her sleep and
softly murmuring to herself. "Thanks to the forethought of Miss Percy, the patient has taken the
most favorable turn."

"Her dreams are happy."

"She is evidently thinking of our friend, the
captain."

"Is his name Geoffrey?" asked Miss Churchill,
dryly. "She is babbling 'Geoffrey', 'dear Geoffrey,' while *his* name is Frank."

CHAPTER XV.

A VISIT AND A DISAPPEARANCE.

AS if guided by a conscience that was free from reproach, Miss Percy deliberately made her exit from the front-door of Woodbine Villa, and quietly stood on the veranda steps to pull on her gloves, although she was aware that her actions were observed by a pair of shrewd eyes from the window above.

"I wish she would follow me," she thought, smiling down on her gloves. "It would be a relaxation to trot her around the village before I faced the ogre. Daring to dictate to me, who could crush her life out by lifting a finger! But I suppose it pays in the long run to be as foolish as they all are, especially since the wise ones are in the minority."

Pausing for a moment to pluck some wild flowers, of which she was passionately fond, she resumed her quiet walk, never once glancing behind to see if she were followed, or even caring to see. She was as calm as if no danger could, by any possibility, overwhelm her; self-assured, self-satisfied and self-respecting. Passing near a certain tree, she glanced at it for a moment with an amused ex-

pression on her face.   A massive branch had fallen
from the parent tree, and now lay cumbering the
ground.

"Her head was hard!" was Miss Percy's comment as she passed on her way.

She entered the secret tunnel, but this time,
when she closed the shell of stone over her, she
fastened it with a massive staple and bar.   Mr.
Newton was impatiently awaiting her in the room
above the vault, and the sight of the fresh flowers
in her hand did not add to his good humor.

"Do you know you have kept me waiting
again?"

"Do *you* know that you are losing your senses, by
speaking of such a trifle?   I was followed, or at
least imagined so, and I acted to throw the spy off
her guard!"

"Is she still active?" he asked with a frown.

"I warned you, and you laughed at my warning,
my uncle!"

"Because you are always warning.   But I de-
tected her meddling fingers last night, in flashing the
wrong signal.   I gave her a lesson."

"It missed its aim; but she ought to be obliged to
you for giving her an excuse for explaining why
one of her shoulders is higher than the other!   A
bruise on the head, a bruise on the shoulder, and
you have one crime less to answer for."

"One crime more if she does not keep out of
my way!   Why were you not in the place to see my
signals?"

" Because I am not allowed. I am suspected and watched. They have a strong suspicion that I have tampered with your friend, Miss Gower ! "

" Curse her ! " interrupted the old man, fiercely. " I wish that it were possible to drag her still lower. I would have killed her but for that hope."

" You are amiable ! " answered Miss Percy calmly. " But to continue : they also suspect, that in some mysterious way I am connected with you. They opened my trunk ! "

" You had nothing there, I hope ? " he asked, sternly.

" It was very likely ! Nothing but the wretched dresses which you avariciously allow me to wear."

" We will speak of that in a moment."

" If I live one of your hours, then, I shall see the end of the world ! " she said, dryly. " But, in sober earnest, I am beginning to be afraid. Even the doctor peeps through the keyhole of my door, and plays the spy to my snores. I have lost my chance with him as with every thing else. It isn't likely he would have a poisoner in his house, especially when he is so rich ! And so I must give up the idea of being Mrs. Dr. Dubois and of riding in my carriage ! "

" So much the better, as you will find it safer to go with me."

" But when *are* you going. The delay makes me as nervous as a woman ! "

" You spoke differently when you were last here ! "

" Because I hoped differently. My one only

absorbing idea now is to get away as soon as possible."

"While I protect you, you idiot, you may defy the world. But my work is done," he said, with a malicious grin, "and I shall probably vanish to-night."

"But how?"

He did not immediately answer her question, but spoke rather as if communing with himself.

"I have forgotten nothing. *She* is brought down from pride to degradation, more dishonored and vile than she feared to be. A public by-word, a blot, an ulcer, a scab, every thing that she deserves to be! To-morrow, despite the efforts of her friends, the newspapers will receive her name, and the next day the immoral woman of local fame will be known through the country as a murderess. Let them help it if they can!"

"But if she disproves this?"

"She is welcome, if *she can!* But the stigma is attached to her; she is degraded in her own proud eyes; she will writhe and shrink under the torment, whether she is doomed to hang, or whether she lives to infinity. That is all I care. Her fame, for which she so foolishly fought, is besmirched, blasted irrevocably; I have made her life a hell, and she is welcome to live in it or die in it, even though I have blasted my own soul in conquering her!"

The handsome face was contorted with vindictive

passion till it might have served as the portrait of a fiend.

"Having done so much, you mean to remain here?"

"Having done so much, I am exulting in it; exulting in the knowledge that, even if she escapes the rope, she will be penniless in her isolation. What money remains I take with me; the branded harlot and murderess will starve!"

"*You* are wasting the time now," said Miss Percy, impatiently. "The point that most concerns me is, how am I going to save my own neck?"

"You have decided to go with me?"

"The prospect is not attractive, but I can't help myself," she answered, with a shrug of the shoulders.

"The yacht will come here to-night."

"I thought you had sent it away."

"You idiot!" he hissed. "I tell you the yacht will be here to-night. It will anchor out in the river; but at a signal it will send a boat to shore to take us away."

"But how am I to bring my trunk?"

"Worse than idiot! it is not a time to think of such matters. Take a few necessary articles, meet me here, and leave the rest to me."

"I hope we are not going to have *him* as a companion," said Miss Percy, significantly.

"*He* leaves as we enter!" answered the old man, with a harsh laugh. "With a weight at his heels, I send him to his friends."

" After your promise ? " she asked, with a frown.

" My promise was not to harm a hair of his head. I will keep the promise. I surrender him to the fishes unhurt ! Do you object, my lady Innocence ? "

" Again I am powerless."

" And again I warn you to cast aside your stupid prejudices. You had a taste once of my opinion on that score. I will not tolerate a weakness on your part ; but I will assist you in a revenge. If you feel like giving the doctor a lesson, invite him here, or lure him here, and I will blow him up with the rest of the building ! "

" Why do this ? "

" As a display of fireworks at my departure ! I should have brought the cursed woman here, did I not prefer that she should live ! "

" What is that strange noise ? " asked Miss Percy, nervously.

The noise sounded like faint, muffled cries for help ; as of a person struggling with suffocation.

" That is an obstinate friend of mine saying his prayers ! He knows more than is good for him, and he is a part of the fireworks."

" Your humor is grimmer than usual to-day ! You must be happy ! "

" I am ! Bring your doctor here and try me. Or the spy who escaped from my clutches ! And take a warning for yourself ; remain firm to the last, and I am your friend ; and by the blood that stains my hand I promise to take you with me at any cost,

and let you live in luxury ! Utter one word of
treachery, or lead me to believe you intend to utter
it, and I will dash out your brains, even though it
costs me my life ! You know what I have done ;
you know what I can do ! "

" It isn't likely that I should play the traitor at
the last moment, with nothing to gain but a jail or
worse ! " she answered, contemptuously.

" I fear your moods of sentimental innocence ! "

" They died the moment you took me in hand !
What hopes has a poisoner, even when playing
the part of traitor ? They *know* me to be such, and
what mercy can I expect from them ? Less even
than from you."

" I will keep my word to you."

" It is amusing to think so, since you are all on
whom I am to depend ! At what time to-night am
I to meet you here ? "

" Between eleven and twelve. The yacht will be
here at the latter hour ; or, perhaps, a little later ;
but here it will be ! "

" But if we should be surprised."

" We will be all blown up with the tower, my
sweet ; remember that ! " he said, with a
malicious grin. " Remember that ! Remember
that ! "

" You are still harping on the old subject," she
answered wearily. " I did not blame you before,
but at this late hour it is ridiculous ! How shall
we go out ? "

" By the secret tunnel to the shore. What I wish

to take away is already there, what I leave behind—
my curses—the woman is welcome to."

The old man repeated his directions, carefully,
elaborately ;   and   the   changes   that   might   be
necessary in change of circumstances.   His final
directions and intentions he whispered in a low
voice, as if fearing even the stone walls might
hear.   She listened with earnest, intelligent face,
and, at times, her wit anticipated his words.   At
the end of a half hour she left him, and emerged
from the gloom into the open air.

" I   suppose this is called seeing life ! " she
exclaimed, after bidding the old man farewell, and
while inhaling the fresh, exhilarating air.   " Cain
was the first murderer ; I wonder who will have the
credit of being the last !   And I could treat my
good doctor to a dose of gunpowder !   Let him
pursue my shrinking coyness to the secret tower,
and when the foolish beast dreamed of his triumph
spring the mine, and let his soul loose !   It is
tempting, but I fear a trifle out of my line ! "

She laughed nervously, and after walking a little
distance, seated herself by the wayside and pressed
her hands to her head.   She was the one living
figure in the autumn landscape ;   an insignificant
spot of color against the huge tree under which
she was sitting.

Mechanically she gathered a few of the brightly
colored fallen leaves, and held them idly in her
hand.

" This is my sentimental innocence," she murmured bitterly. "Always alone, always without love, always without sympathy. I wish I were somebody else. I suppose the doctor would call this remorse. The doctor! The doctor! Even that is hateful to me now!"

She tossed the leaves to the ground and stared abstractedly down on them. Suddenly she smiled: "I will keep away the tears by thinking of the gunpowder!"

She rose, but before going homeward, she walked to the railway station and sent a telegraphic message.

"It is still remorse!" she murmured, while filling out the blank. "Always remorse, with desolation as my reward!"

The message was directed to "Captain Frank Travers, 53 X—— Avenue, N—— City!"

Miss Churchill, in the meantime, was enjoying an interesting conversation with Mr. Terms.

The old lawyer had received her with great affability; and when she disclosed her profession and her desires, expressed himself as willing to share his knowledge with her to the utmost.

"As I told Detective Sharpe yesterday, Miss Churchill, I started with the idea that Mr. Addison was the victim of a heartless crime, and I still cling to the belief, though I have modified my opinion. I rejoice that, for the honor of your sex, events have demonstrated that the party whose hands are stained with blood is *not* a female. I'm now persuaded that my client was murdered for his

money, and that a certain dependent is the murderer. It is also demonstrated beyond doubt that
my client was a sensualist, and that a reckless indul-
gence in wine, women and speculation knocked the
foundation from under a very noble fortune. The
fortune *is* dissippated, but notwithstanding this
fact, there is still a good sum of money and
some very valuable articles of convertible property,
which would pay an evil-hearted man for a crime,
still to be accounted for. Without waste of words,
Miss Churchill, these are the conclusions I have
reached after investigation and study: I believe
master and man were bound together by the closest
ties, but whereas the master's tie was that of love,
the man's tie was that of self-interest. Detective
Sharpe told me yesterday that in the doctor's opinion
Addison was poisoned, and that in addition he had
not only found the drug-store where the poison was
purchased, but he has also identified the man who
purchased it, and that man, Miss Churchill, was Max
Newton. Max Newton is the guilty party, and he
intends to arrest him at the earliest opportunity."

" Then we are all agreed at last ? " said Miss
Churchill, with a sigh of relief.

" Should the scoundrel vanish——"

" You may be sure that the wretch will not
escape. Detective Sharpe, with all his faults, is not
a man to suffer that ; neither is he unwise enough to
strike before he is sure of his game. I am so satisfied of that, that I intend to leave the arrest to my
confrère and busy myself with another matter.

every thing is now satisfactory, except a link in the chain of evidence. This I will supply by going to the city myself. My presence will be more valuable there than here. May I ask for the liberty of writing a note here ? "

"Certainly, madam, certainly," said Mr. Terms, with great gallantry. " My desk is at your disposal."

Miss Churchill wrote the following letter :

" DEAR DR. DUBOIS :

" Every thing is so satisfactoryhere that I intend to run down to the city, to personally look after the yacht *Oriana.* Detective Sharpe is on the right track at last, and I leave the arrest of the criminal to him—out of courtesy to his sex ! There is nothing for you to do in my absence, but keep a sharp look-out on Miss Percy, and get your patient in a speaking condition as soon as possible. I would see you for a moment, but time is valuable. I go immediately to the city, and shall not return until to-morrow noon at earliest. In an emergency, which is hardly probable, consult with Detective Sharpe."

Miss Churchill signed and sealed the letter.

" Is it possible to send this note to Dr. Dubois at Woodbine Villa right away ? It is important ! "

" I will attend to it. My office-boy will take it immediately to its destination."

With her usual forethought, Miss Churchill

waited until she saw the messenger depart on his mission, and then, with a light heart, boarded the train at the little station, and was whirled toward the great city.

CHAPTER XVI.

LIGHT AND DARKNESS.

MISS CHURCHILL'S letter increased, instead of diminishing, the doctor's perplexity ; its reference to Detective Sharpe was a worry and a puzzle at the same time; for in obedience to orders he had called at Lesbia Villa and had been told that the detective had also gone to the city for fresh evidence.

" And *she* is said to be an acute reasoner and crime-detecter !" exclaimed the doctor, gazing contemptuously at the letter. " She goes away believing every thing is right, while to me, every thing is in confusion. And *I, I* am to do nothing ! She scorns *my* assistance. So be it ! But I will not hold myself responsible for the results. When she fails, in her foolish impetuosity, she will remember me and science ! "

In the invalid's room a curious scene was being acted.

Miss Percy had approached the bed to discover that Miss Gower was awake and tranquil. She greeted her maid with a smile.

" You feel better ? "

" Better and stronger, but very much perplexed.

Was it the old horror, or have I been dreaming?"

"Wait until you are stronger."

"Help me to think, my dear, as you have helped me to live."

It would have surprised the wise doctor had he witnessed the scene from some secret retreat. If there were any humiliation, it was on the side of the mistress; she clasped the maid's hand, glanced up to her face with an affection and admiration that were unaccountable, considering the difference in her social position. Stranger still, there was an air of quiet protection in Miss Percy's affectionate manner, such as a mother would have displayed in humoring a wayward child. Remorse would not have explained the puzzle, even when backed by scientific syllogism.

"I should have died without your tenderness, my dear, and it is so strange ! I can look into your face without any shame."

"Your inferiors can do it also !" said Miss Percy, with a little grimace.

"Do they know ?" asked the invalid, with a flush on her pale face.

"They know nothing ; they are too clever for that ! They do every thing according to quadratic equations and evolution, and they are as wise as they deserve to be ! But you must not speak any more now ; in a little while you will know every thing. Yet if you must have a punishment, I will inform you that Captain Travers is as dangerously in love as ever ! As to the rest, the clouds have all vanished, and I think we shall see the sun at last. You shall have a glimpse of it now."

Miss Percy drew back the curtains, and the mild, golden, autumn sunlight flooded the room. Miss Percy, standing near the window, was surrounded by it as by an extravagant glory.

"The wise men intend to question you to-day," she said, again approaching the bed, "and you will need all your strength to resist weariness. You must speak of the old life for your own vindication, and then you can forget it forever ! "

" You are in no danger, my dear ? "

" Only such as it amuses me to face. When it suits me, I shall get out of it. It is curious how foolish wise people are ! " she concluded, reflectively.

" If I do not speak it, dear, I am none the less grateful."

" I only want your unspoken gratitude. Words are very wicked things. If I were only rich enough, I would found a kingdom of dumb people, and it should be all men ! Sleep now, that I may prepare you when you wake for the grand reception of philosophers ! "

" I prefer to hear your voice."

" Fortunately, you will not hear Miss Churchill's just at present, and that is a consolation. I wish I had been all they thought me for her sake ! As to my voice, I am dumb until you again wake up ! "

"Remember while waiting, dear, that I have entered a new life," said the invalid, sadly.

"Marriage!" thought Miss Percy. "If she has done any thing wrong, she will be more than punished. If I were a cruel law-maker, instead of punishing a woman with imprisonment, I would give her a husband!"

She quietly busied herself about the room until her mistress had fallen asleep.

Glancing down at the unconscious figure, she continued her criticisms.

"For her sake I think it would have been better the other way. And she is the only one who has been disinterestedly kind to me ; the only one who would feel real regret if disaster overwhelmed me. How I can escape it I can't see just now. But it must be done!"

She sighed drearily.

"Fortunately, life isn't so very attractive ; I have seen enough of it. If a fairy would grant me one favor now, I should ask for forgetfulness!"

She retired to her room and burned all her papers, as if she were presiding at her own funeral ; then sat near the window, and fell into a deep reverie.

Later in the afternoon she again entered her mistress's room, brought her food, and prepared her to receive company.

"When the doctor comes, make him your confidant, and let him tell it to the others if he pleases. But say nothing of me, or of any thing but your wretched experiences in that wretched house. It is necessary to tell that, and that only. But flatter the hero's vanity by allowing him to believe that he is drawing you out. Men require to be treated in that way. Appeal to their vanity, and they will bray in any key you select! You will understand my reason later."

"I require nothing but your advice. You are strong; I am weak. But you will desert me?"

"I would not miss the doctor's science-primer deductions for all the world. I deserve that luxury, at least!"

And yet she welcomed him in a manner that was almost affectionate, and flushed when his eagle eyes were cast in her direction.

"I am rejoiced to see that you are better, Miss Gower," he said, seating himself near the bed.

"I am better, sir, thanks to your skill. I feel so strong that I think I could leave my bed."

"We will try that expedient to-morrow. In the meantime allow me to say a few words. There is a subject which it is necessary to discuss. That is, certain information which you could give would throw light on a matter that now perplexes us. I believe I have your confidence?"

"And my gratitude, doctor."

"Very good! Now I should like to test this confidence, for your own welfare. What you tell me in your impulsive womanly way, I could arrange with the cold precision of science, and deliver it in a manner that would be least jarring on your feelings. But at the start, let me assure you there is

nothing to fear. Your enemy is out of the way
of doing any further harm. He is dead!"

Miss Gower sighed heavily, but from the expression of her face the news was not displeasing.

" When you are stronger you shall hear all the
details ; at present, you must suppress your curiosity, and be content to answer me blindly."

" Question me, then ! "

" You were an adopted child. How were you
treated in your new home ? "   .

" By my adopted father and mother with unfailing love and tenderness. In all the long years I
lived with them they acted toward me as the angels
they were ! "

" And their son ? "

" Their son was a fiend ! " said Miss Gower,
flashing into anger at the remembrance. " The
devil must have stolen the real child, and placed
a fiend in its cradle ! He was a hypocrite as a child ;
pinching me, tearing out my hair, and plunging
pins into me in the nursery, and showing the most
sanctimonious face out of it ! He was assisted in all
his fiendishness, and taught new fiendishness, by a
servant friend of his, one Max Newton ! "

" I already have my eyes on that gentleman ! "
said the doctor, severely.

" My childish life was one long torture, and had
it not been for my love for my adopted parents, I
would have broken away from it ! But even as a
child I saw that their lives were centered in their
son ; he was their idol, and remained so, I hope, to

the end. At least, if they ever had a glimpse of the truth it was not from me ; for as a child I vowed that they should never suffer a pang on my account, and what I vowed as a child I kept as a woman. My lips were closed until they rested quietly in their graves."

" And as man and woman ? "

" His vices increased with age. I had been adopted with the intention of ultimately becoming his wife ; but when we were old enough to speak on such subjects, he amused himself by insulting an innocent shrinking girl with the announcement that he never intended to marry, which was an old-fashioned invention of stupidity ; but had made up his mind to lead a life of liberty. He repeated this again and again ; forcing me to listen to his plans for the future. He endeavored to make me read vile books, which his friend Max Newton supplied him with. In fact, his one unfailing delight was to bring the blush of shame to my cheeks, and the tears of humiliation to my eyes. I think that even his blindly loving parents suspected him at last ; for they changed my room to one near their own, and my kind adopted mother kept me near her protecting presence. But at every opportunity the wretch persecuted me, vowing, at the same time, if I revealed one word of what he said, that he would rob me of the love that sheltered me. I feared him, for his energy in carrying out a wicked plot was only equal to his cunning in inventing it. Even as a boy, in some fancied spite against him, he would

deliberately bruise himself with a hammer or other
weapon, and then complain to his parents that I
had done it ! That he did not cut and mutilate himself was only due to the fact that he had an insane
horror of blood. Conceive many years passed in
these tortures, and you may guess at my life ; but
not at my sufferings ! "

" He was undoubtedly insane," said the doctor,
"and had he not died, would have ended his days
in an asylum."

" I was comparatively safe until his parents
died, but on the very day they were buried he cast
aside the last remnant of manhood, and suggested
to me a mode of life which to think of even now
fills me with horror and shame. On that very day
I left his house, never to enter it again. Before
their death, his parents had personally delivered to
me a little sum of money, ample for all my wants.
I hired a cottage, placed it in charge of a kind
old lady, and lived in it. But he persecuted
me even here. When I ordered him away, he
swore he would be revenged, and rushed off only
to return again. As he lost hope, he gained in
fiendishness, and the last time I saw him he vowed
that he would not die, till he had degraded me in
the eyes of the world, even if he devoted his entire
fortune to it. I would say that his servant Max
Newton was equally vindictive. This man was paid
for humoring his master's vices, and he had been
promised a large sum if he could persuade me to
accept his master's proposals. Failing in this, he

also swore to degrade me ; and I feared the evil servant more than I feared the evil master ! That I am strong, doctor, is proved by the fact that I can tell you these things without shrieks or tears ! The horror has weighed on me like a nightmare ; for a long year the fear of this revenge has robbed me of sleep, of happiness, of hope ! What I suffered in the house with him, is nothing compared with the agonies I have suffered since I left it. With horrors accumulating around me, innocent as I was, with no hopes of escaping from them, I should perhaps have become as reckless and as degraded as he wished me—"

" Had it not been that you were too sensible to allow an idiot to rob you of your pride and common-sense," interrupted Miss Percy. Then turning to the doctor, she added :

" He was a bad man, doctor ! "

" A wretch ! " nodded the doctor, with an expression of disgust on his face.

" No chivalry there, sir, toward a weak, helpless sex. No offers of protection ; no high ideas of morality ; no anxiety as to the present condition of the church ! Yes, doctor, *you* have the right to call him a wretch ! "

The doctor was a novice in this species of hero-worship ; and he eyed Miss Percy with marked perplexity.

" Men are sometimes born demons," he said, first coughing to clear his throat. " You have told me, Miss Gower, all that I have a right to know——"

"And she is tired out by the labor," again interrupted Miss Percy, with strange authoritativeness in the presence of her mistress and her hero. "Has she not said enough for to-day? To-morrow she may be able to give in detail the facts, which you, in the cause of science, are so anxious to hear. Better still, sir, she may whisper them to me, and *I* will retail them to you in the library to-night."

The doctor did not admire Miss Percy in her new mood. She was already presuming on the protection that she had not yet received. It is certain that she was lacking in delicacy. He presented a frowning profile to her, and honored Miss Gower with his attentions.

"My interest in this matter, Miss Gower, is of an impersonal nature. I am working in the cause of justice, and what you have told me was necessary to a clear understanding of a subject in which I am interested. In the cause of friendship, I may have something else to ask ; but in the absence of my colleague, and also considering your weak condition, I will defer it, with other matters, until to-morrow ! "

Twilight passes rapidly into night in September, and the sunlight had long since faded out of the room. When the doctor departed, it was still light enough to see the figure on the bed. In the increasing darkness, the figure was invisible, and silent in sleep. The moonlight was visible through the openings in the curtains, but here there were no

eyes to appreciate its mellow softness. Mr. Morris
and doctor Dubois are socially chatting over a glass
of wine in the library. Through the quiet autumn
evening the church bell is pealing the hour of ten.

Miss Percy in traveling attire, and small valise
in hand, pauses in the open air to count the strokes
of the bell, and then continues on her journey.
She deserts her trunk without a sigh, but before
leaving the house she has softly kissed her sleeping
mistress on the forehead.

It is a beautiful star-light night, without a breath
of wind ; the crickets are still recalling summer as
they chirrup from the trees and bushes ; and the
dead leaves suggesting winter are invisible, but
she hears them crackle under her feet.

The quietness of the night quiets her nervousness
and the warmth returns to her cold cheeks. She
is unusually interested in the things around her ; a
criminal doomed to life-long imprisonment would
have felt the same interest. In front of her, in the
distance, is a spread of waters with a line of quivering moonlight moving with the ripples. Half in
idleness, half in wonder, she walks onward, from
right to left, from left to right, changing her point
of view ; but the line of quivering light changes
with her. The doctor would have solved the mystery for her. She does not think of him ; but of
the far-back days when she and the world were
younger, and the moonlighted waters offered the
same puzzle to her childish eyes. It was only a
momentary glimpse of a long-dead world ; but it

quickened her breath, tingled her nerves, and brought the moisture to her eyes.

A quiet night, with all the familiar objects bathed in a tender light, assuming their most attractive appearance, as if anxious to appear at their best in bidding a companion farewell. She had nearly reached her journey's end ; yet she hesitated before completing it, turning from the narrow, black tunnel, to enjoy one last look at the clear blue sky and the motionless trees. Her face was thoughtful and sad ; and the moonlight repeated its old mystery in the two tears that welled up from her eyes and rolled down her cheeks. When she turned from the light above to the darkness beneath her, her face changed, and what was yearning tenderness became stern resolution.

In her absence the stone room in the tower had undergone a change. A rare Persian rug partially covered the floor, and on this was standing a rarer table, that had formerly ornamented the drawing-room. Two richly-covered arm-chairs stood beside the table, and seated in the largest was Mr. Max Newton, with a grim smile of satisfaction on his face.

" You are earlier than I expected, ma belle ! "

" I was fearful, and dreaded some trouble. I could not wait longer."

" You are welcome ; for I was a little lonely myself. I prepared this room for your reception."

" You are very kind, but it is a waste of time. If you had only provided a little supper and a little wine to make the time pass pleasantly, I could better have appreciated your thoughtfulness."

" You shall have all the wine you can drink, ma belle, and all the food you can eat ! We will drink to the health of the old house before we send it to the skies ! The clockwork is already set, and started in the cavern, and after we have left the house will vanish ! "

" That is very comfortable ! I hope you have not made any mistake with your clockwork, to treat us to a premature explosion ! "

" By the color not flying from your cheeks, I see that you have not lost confidence in me ! Ah, ma belle, if human life were only longer, I would conquer the world."

" Is your friend still saying his prayers, uncle ? I don't hear him move."

" Probably he is absorbed in making his will ! " answered Mr. Newton, with a diabolical grin. " What shall we drink his health in ? Make your choice, for I am sorry to say, even the wine-cellar will not be saved."

" I leave it to you, uncle. But I wish you could give me something to eat. I haven't touched any thing since morning, and I am chilled too ! "

" Place these dishes and glasses on the table and wait for me," said the old man, pointing to the corner of the room, and then disappearing down the staircase.

Before obeying, Miss Percy took a small bottle

from her valise and placed it in the bosom of her dress.

The old man returned with a salver, on which were several articles of food and three black bottles.

" We must be satisfied with cold fare to-night, ma belle, but before we leave, we will heat some water and thaw our blood with brandy. Drink, drink even to intoxication, if you like. I will take care of you for the amusement it will cause me. Serve yourself to the food, and if you are in the mood, empty the bottle of madeira ! "

Mr. Newton carefully wiped his plate and washed out his wine glass, and then drank more than he ate.

" Is every thing ready, uncle ? "

" Every thing, my lady light-head ! Satisfy your senses and leave thinking to me. Amuse me with the tattle of our friends."

" I am to be arrested to-morrow, uncle," said Miss Percy, with a smile; " arrested as a poisoner of my dear mistress ; and, when he is caught, Geoffrey Draper is to be tried for murder. Isn't it curious that they never once suspected you ? "

" One fool did begin to suspect me, and for that act of superhuman wisdom his body will give *éclat* to the explosion in our honor. But what of the woman ? "

" She is regarded as a partner, in more senses than one, of her lover, Mr. Draper ! "

" She shall live after this, live if she outlasts

the world !   If I am forgotten elsewhere, I shall sur-
vive in her memory !   And that is a species of fame
I hunger for.   Her virtue !   If she had been less
of a fool, he would have grown tired of her in a
week, and she might have gone her way and
married whom she pleased, and no one cared about
it or her !   Fool !   she deserves to suffer.   Drink,
ma belle, drink yourself into liveliness !   Take the
check off your tongue, and speak to me as if I
were a young man ! "

"It is difficult, uncle, with chattering teeth.
Warm my blood, and I promise to be amusing ! "

"You have the family failing, and prefer something stronger than wine.   I am prepared even for
this emergency ! "

He lighted a small oil-stove, over which he
placed a pan of water.

"When *he* was away, I lived in this little room for
weeks together, and yonder little stove supplied all
my wants.   Light the other candles, ma belle, we
will have a feast ! "

He half filled two goblets with the hot water,
and placed one of them on the table in front of Miss
Percy.   While he was busied with the stove, she
drew the bottle from the bosom of her dress
and poured a portion of its clear contents into *her
own glass*, and then hastily secreted the bottle.
She then stretched her arm across the table ; but
hastily withdrew it as the old man turned round.
A wicked smile came to his lips.

"Squeeze a little lemon in your glass, ma belle,

and I will squeeze a little lemon into mine. Now pour this dose of brandy into your glass and I will pour this whisky into mine. Are you ready, ma belle? " he asked with fierce joviality.

" I am ready, uncle, even to the sugar."

" Then, ma belle, we will change glasses in loving confidence! Hand me your goblet, sweetheart." He laughed harshly as the exchange was made; duped by his own suspicions, as the wise Miss Percy had foreseen and prepared for! She submitted to the change of glasses with so much innocent direct-ness, that he felt ashamed of his doubts.

" Your health, ma belle," he said gayly, drinking from the prepared glass. " I hope this will melt your icy blood and free your tongue. Drink! drink! And talk to me as if I were a woman and your friend. Tell me about the doctor, and how much money you squeezed out of him."

" I owe him nothing, uncle," she answered dryly.

" Then tell me how much he owes you!" continued Mr. Newton with a short laugh.

" He owes me nothing, uncle!"

" It was, then, love after all?"

" You are making the mistake you made once before. You are blind on the side of decency, uncle."

" Be careful, ma belle, be careful. I am a free man again. I have plenty of time at my disposal now, and if it becomes my humor to again hammer down your will and obstinacy, I won't fail this

time. Drink, you little devil," he continued, empty-
ing his own glass and refilling it. " Loose your
wits ; I will keep mine ! I could empty a wine-
cellar without losing my senses ! "

In truth, alcohol, instead of rendering Mr. Newton helpless, only intensified his eccentricities. His
brain remained clear ; but the muddy pool of his
emotional nature was stirred, and its sediment
universally diffused. Miss Percy's opinion of her
venerable relative may be inferred from the fact
that she kept her hand in the pocket of her dress ;
the slender fingers clutching the handle of a
pistol.

" How are we to know when the yacht arrives,
uncle ? "

" We leave this place at twelve, and wait for it
hidden near the shore—I have a prettier niece
than I imagined ! Your health, ma belle." The
hand holding out the glass had lost its steadiness,
and the liquid in the glass spattered the table.
" Come—come—come and kiss me !" He stammered in his speech ; paused, and over his face
there passed a wave of malignant hatred.

" You——" he hissed fiercely, yet feebly.

For the first time in the interview Miss Percy
felt at ease ; she withdrew her hand from her pocket
and calmly consulted her watch. " It was time ! "
she murmured, glancing at the old man who was
sinking into passiveness in his chair, yet even in
his impotency grinding his teeth and feebly clench-
ing his hand.

" If I had time I would box his ears for his insults;
but wanting time I shall surrender him to a friend
who will be only too anxious to pay him his
respects ! "

She opened his coat and extracted from its inner
pocket a sealed envelope ; and with a contemptuous shrug of the shoulders left the room.

" Another victim of too much cleverness," she
muttered.   " And still another is waiting my foolishness for assistance."

She pushed open the heavy door and entered the
large vaulted chamber. Securely tied, hands and
feet, and with a gag in his mouth, lay the redoubt-
able Detective Sharpe.

Miss Percy was too much disturbed by her own
thoughts to enjoy the humorous spectacle. She
removed the gag ; loosened the bonds, and the
disconsolate and numbed detective rose slowly and
painfully to his feet.

" I'm much obliged to you, Miss Percy," he said,
humbly.   " But if I once get hold——"

" Excuse me, Mr. Sharpe, but neither of us has
time to pay or to receive compliments. The man
you seek is in the room below this ; but the tower
is undermined and will be blown in the air after
midnight. There is no time to explain. Listen,
and obey. There are still fifteen minutes of
safety ! Have you any men around ? "

" There is, or was, one in the veranda."

" Well summon him, return here with him, and
then remove the senseless man. Get him out of

the house, and yourself out of the house, all within
fifteen minutes ! Do you hear ? "

" Yes, but I don't understand."

" If you understood you would again make a fool
of yourself," she said, dryly. " Listen and obey.
The man is in the room below, and you have less
than fifteen minutes to act. Go ! This way ; and
return this way ! "

She pulled back the door opening on the hall,
and secured it from springing forward.

" Go, now, for help, and receive the merited
honor of capturing the murderer ! Remember that
every moment is precious."

" I understand," said the detective, rushing into
the hall, " and if I'm caught *this* time, I deserve to
be blown up ! "

She listened for a moment to his retreating footsteps, and then returned to the room below, but not
to wait. After casting one contemptuous glance at
the sleeping man, she pushed against a projection
in the wall. One of the stones slipped aside,
thereby revealing a high but narrow opening.

" If I only knew where the explosive is I would
remove it. *My* mistake ; but it can not be reme-
died now, and there is time even for a fool to act !"

She entered the narrow passage-way, and the
stone closed behind her. A narrow passage-way,
darker than the night outside it, with a flight of
steps and a perceptible slope, with mysterious
puffs of air blowing into it from secret openings. A
long, carefully-constructed passage-way, costing

years to build and the work of a madman!
Miss Percy sped through the darkness as if
she were well acquainted with the ground.
Having passed straight forward for a certain
distance, with her hand touching the walls, she
turned to the right, and, in a moment, entered
the aneurism of a cave into which the artery
dilated. Touching a spring, she entered a
broader cave, and the sea, glittering in the moonlight, was before her.

She glanced anxiously about; but no yacht
was in sight. Ships were at rest on the water with
furled sails; but not the yacht she sought. She
glanced at her watch in the moonlight. Two minutes to twelve!

Suppose she had been suspected! Suppose she
should reach the yacht too late! Suppose a thousand possibilities! a thousand impossibilities! a
thousand horrors! every thing! any thing! The
passiveness frenzied her. She could have con-
trolled her feelings to the end if she had plunged
from activity into activity. But to stand idle with
the goal in view, to——

There was a strange tremor of the earth! She felt
before she heard. She covered her ears with her
hands and shrieked. It was coming! Yes, with the
faint sound of the midnight bell, it came! A flash
of fire, and a loud explosion, causing the very rocks
to shiver!

That was over! She panted with terror, yet
smiled in her relief. Again she glanced over the

water and saw *her* yacht, as if it had dropped from the clouds.

A small boat had emerged from its shadow, and was speeding in her direction. It touched the sand and she leaped into it.

"Take me first to the yacht, and then return with all your men!" she said to the man in the stern. "*He* is in the cave, and he needs· you all. Quick!"

She spoke commandingly, and they obeyed with energy.

"What was the explosion, Miss Percy?"

"The house has vanished. It blew up before he expected; and he fears the report will bring the enemies on him! You must be quick, and take your guns with you. There is a world of riches to share among you!"

Pulled by the sturdy arms, the boat flew through the water. It reached the yacht, and Miss Percy was the first to climb to its deck.

A whispered conversation, a slight pause, and then two boats emerged from the shadow of the yacht, and hastened toward the shore.

Miss Percy was in action again; it was the one stimulation she needed! She passed through the cabin of the yacht, unfastened a door at the other end, and entered a small, dark room; too dark for its interior to be seen. Not a sound was to be heard.

"Geoffrey!" she called, with a nervous tremor in her voice. "Geoffrey!"

All was silent. More activity, or she would fall into unconsciousness !

" Geoffrey ! Geoffrey ! "

" Eh ? what ? " asked a voice from the darkness.

" Thank God ! " she murmured, with her hand clasped to her heart. " Geoffrey, where are you ? I dare not light a lamp, or they will see it from the outside. 'Where are you ? "

" Tied, neck and heels, on the bed, ready for the fishes ! " answered a cheery voice. " But not a bit afraid, having faith in a good angel."

She entered the darkness, and with extended hands, groped her way. It was a small room, and she easily reached the bed.

" If I hurt, tell me. I must sever your bonds in the dark."

" Cut away, angel ; I will stand it ! "

With intelligence at the ends of her fingers, she cautiously severed the ropes that were twisted around a human form ; then emerged from the darkness into the light, followed by a handsome young man, who had evidently endured much suffering.

" I hoped that friends would have met us, as I warned them. But they are all idiots, and we must depend on ourselves. Are you strong enough to swim ? "

" Ready to risk it, or any thing, to smell the air of freedom again ! "

" Well, creep through the window and swim to the shore. It is not far."

"And you?"

"I will remain; I do not fear!"

"But I do! I will not leave you at this moment, weak as I am, and strong as you are! They will have to step over my body first!"

"Escape! They are already returning, frenzied by my falsehood. Escape! It is a fitting end!"

"Too romantic, by half, Miss Percy! I am not hero enough to let you suffer."

"But listen, they are on the deck."

"Evidently cracking each other's skulls, Miss Percy. Do you hear the groans and curses?"

"It is Captain Travers," she said, joyfully. "He has come in time!"

The tension had proved too great, even for her, and as Captain Travers rushed into the cabin she uttered a sigh, and fell unconscious to the ground.

CHAPTER XVII.

DISCOVERED AT LAST !

THE principal morning paper in the city thus commented on the events of the evening before in Cypressville :

"As the finger of time pointed to midnight, Cypressville was treated to another sensation ; an attempt was made to blow up Lesbia Villa, the scene of the late tragedy. Fortunately, it was unsuccessful ; the house is undamaged save for a few broken windows and cracked ceilings. The reason for the attempt was a villain's desire to destroy Mr. Sharpe, the pride of our detectives, who escaped from a vile attempt to ruin him, that another laurel leaf may ornament his modest brow ! Just before the explosion, he was in the house maturing his plans for the capture of the criminal who had murdered the ill-fated Mr. Addison. From the very start his subtile brain, which far excels in cunning those of the famed detectives of fiction, had pierced through the maze of mystery, and reached its nucleus ! Like a sleuth-hound, he steadily pursued the trail, and had finally planted his fangs in the throat of the quarry. In the cause of justice, we have hitherto refrained from com-

menting on the case ; but the reasons for silence
are removed, and we can now freely state, that
Max Newton is the man who has stained his hands
with a noble master's blood. To Detective Sharpe,
and to him alone, is due the credit of this discovery ;
and that the prisoner is not now in jail is owing
to the fact that he mysteriously disappeared at the
very moment the detective intended to arrest him.
Detective Sharpe escaped by a miracle ; he was
grappling with the frenzied criminal a few minutes
before the explosion, and had bound him. The
wretch refused to move and the detective rushed
out to obtain assistance. At that moment the
explosion occurred, fortunately, as we have said,
doing little harm. The detective, followed by the
devoted Mr. Tomlins, rushed back into the building ; but the murderer had escaped. He had cut
his bonds and by means of a secret passage reached
the sea-shore, where, doubtless, a boat was waiting
for him. We venture this statement from the fact
that three police officers were picked up out of the
water. They had been placed over-night, by Captain Travers, in charge of the yacht *Oriana*, which
they had bravely captured and rescued a prisoner
from it. Trusting in the majesty of their shields
and batons, they were quietly walking on deck when
they were seized by the crew whom they were
guarding, and were unceremoniously pitched over-
board. The yacht has disappeared with the
murderer, but Sharpe is on the trail !

" The details of Sharpe's heroic act, and of the

secret passages in the house, will be found in another
column. We erect public monuments to our war-
riors, poets and statesmen ; we patronize our liter-
ary men and our artists ; can nothing be done for
our brave detectives ? We have opened a subscrip-
tion bureau that Detective Sharpe may receive the
public approbation that he merits. Every thing
will be received, from the artisans' penny to the
millionaire's check for thousands. We head the
list with our own mite. Let the ball roll ! "

Miss Percy read this enthusiastic narrative in
her own room ; read it and read it again, and
nearly laughed herself into convulsions.

"It isn't every tragedy that ends as a farce,"
was her amusing comment. "Detective Sharpe
ran away to escape our laughter, and not on account
of the criminals. As for my good relative, the
devil has again helped him—the devil and Mr.
Sharpe ! He is too cunning to be caught now, and
I was a fool to trust any body but myself. They
all went wrong but me, wise as they are ! But I'm
abnormal, as the doctor would say. The beast
doctor ! We are still to hear his wise comments."

Miss Percy descended to the drawing-room,
where were her mistress, looking very pale but not
unhappy ; Doctor Dubois, Mr. Morris, Geoffrey
Draper, and the good-natured, smiling Captain
Travers. At the moment the maid entered the
room, the doctor had finished reading aloud the
newspaper item that had so amused her.

"This is the value of fame ! " he exclaimed,

throwing the newspaper aside. "I am not vain, and the thing is a trifle in itself ; but if truth must be told, what success Sharpe met with is due to me. He was on the wrong track, until science demonstrated to him that Max Newton was the guilty man !"

The doctor paused to turn toward Geoffrey Draper, who was in danger of suffocation in his attempt to suppress his laughter.

"Excuse me, doctor," he said, unable longer to restrain himself, and laughing until he was purple in the face. "The whole business is sad ; but hang me it *is* so funny !"

Again he gave way to his mirth, and the sympathetic Miss Percy kept him company, to the indignation of the grave doctor.

Mr. Draper again apologized, and when he had conquered his sense of the humorous, he said :

"May I ask, doctor, if you were convinced that Max Newton was the murderer from the very start ?"

"I *was*, sir, and I *am ;* and I stake my reputation on the truth of this conclusion !"

"I am glad we have got a definite statement at last !" he said, glancing demurely toward the now demure Miss Percy. The doctor retorted with fine sarcasm :

"I hope, sir, you will be able to demonstrate your case as clearly as I could demonstrate *mine!* But we are waiting !"

"I will start the ball," said Miss Percy, taking

her mistress's hand in her own. "I suppose even the stupidest among you is beginning to see that Miss Gower was the victim of a diabolical plot. Two wicked men pursued her, tortured her until I wonder she did not kill herself. *I* would. To gain forgetfulness—"

"I, Oriana Gower, indulged in the vile habit of taking opium, and the habit grew on me till I was a slave !"

"She took opium," said Miss Percy, quietly, "to escape from her agonies. Once, doctor, she waked up in the greatest pain, and at her request I gave her a hypodermic injection of morphine. You saw the mark on her arm and, no doubt, drew some rigid scientific deduction from it !"

The doctor blushed, but made no reply.

"Now, in all that follows, you will always remember that my object was to deceive Max Newton and serve Miss Gower at the same time. If this man once suspected me, disaster would have fallen on myself and on others."

"Poor little thing !" murmured Mr. Draper.

"Before I was a lady's maid, I was enjoying the luxury of starvation. I was desperate, and Mr. Newton took me in hand. He promised me a fabulous sum if I got engaged in Miss Gower's service, and prevented her from speaking until a certain plot was matured. To help myself, and an innocent woman at the same time, I consented to Mr. Newton's proposal, and became a lady's maid."

She paused to softly pat the hand that clasped her own.

"About that time, I think, the very wise Doctor Dubois suspected the truth and spoke to a friend on the subject, to the prejudice of my mistress. To save Miss Gower from the criticism of imbeciles, and also to deceive Mr. Newton, I so acted that every body imagined I was poisoning my mistress. So I allowed her to take opium, thinking, that for a little time at least, oblivion was the best thing for her. On the evening of the day of the murder, I visited the old house, and if Captain Travers had minded his own business, I would have been in possession of a paper that would have destroyed the wicked plot then and there. I knew where this paper was hidden, and could have secured it even in the dark, had not Mr. Draper, who was to have assisted me, whistled a warning, and had not Captain Travers entered the house, opposed my egress, and robbed me of a shawl which *did* belong to Miss Gower. Once again I visited the house, and chloroformed Detective Sharpe, to take from him some letters that Mr. Newton had written, under an anonymous name, to further damage Miss Gower's character. I was fortunate here, for had the detective spoken of his experience to Mr. Newton, my treachery would have been apparent. Mr. Sharpe was a man, and consequently an egoist, and, as the result proved, I wisely trusted to his vanity to conceal his stupidity. When Miss Churchill was summoned, I endeavored to put her

on the right path ; had she invaded my room on
her first appearance, she would have found the
same suggestive letters that she found after a long
delay.   I entered the room where she was watching
to supply Miss Gower with an opium pill, which I
did despite the electric light.   I was anxious to
copy the doctor's report, to see if he were on the
right track, and to emphasize some of his statements
in case of need.   But his science was wiser than
my ignorance, and by fooling me with a false report,
he also fooled justice and himself.   Mr. Draper's
mysterious disappearance at first alarmed me, but
I soon learned from Max Newton that he had been
carried off in the yacht, and so I was compelled to
await his return."

" Do you know any thing of the old cabinet? and
the letters written by Miss Gower to Mr. Addison ? "
asked the doctor.

" I never wrote him any ! " said Miss Gower,
indignantly.

" She never wrote him any," nodded Miss Percy.
" It was one of the many lies invented to ruin
her ! "

" But the cabinet was mutilated."

" Did not Mr. Newton possess an ax !   And
to advance his plot would he hesitate at spoiling
furniture ? "

" And the woman's foot-prints impressed in the
mud ? "

" They were mine ! " said Miss Percy.   " I feared
that the wicked man, with the desire of fixing the

crime past doubt on Miss Gower, would throw about,
here and there, some object or objects belonging
to her. I went, after the storm, and found a brace-
let of hers, which, of course, I picked up and kept.
I made the imprints, but I never thought of the tell-
tale marks at the time."

"But why conceal the matter at all?" persisted
the doctor. "Why not inform justice at once?"

"The flickering candle of your wisdom is blown
out!" answered Miss Percy, with a shrug of the
shoulders. "The crime had been committed, at
least in part, to convict Miss Gower as a murderess.
Every thing pointed to her, and to warn the
authorities would have been to play into the wretch's
hands. For Miss Gower's sake, whose reputation
was in the greatest danger, and for Mr. Draper's
sake, who at any false step of mine was in danger
of death, I had to act with extreme caution. Calling
on the law would have ruined all ; for, Mr. Draper
away, my evidence amounted to nothing. I had to
wait, and I waited. The paper—which had been
removed from its hiding-place—came into my
possession only within a comparatively few hours."

"A little genius!" murmured Mr. Draper to.
himself.

"One trifle more," continued Miss Percy, with
a smile. "Let me freely confess, to my shame, that
in one matter, I *was* guilty. I had the ambition of
becoming the housekeeper and ultimately the wife,
of a very wise man. Dr. Dubois, in his nobility of
soul, will understand me when I say that the ambi-

tion no longer exists, and that, in my opinion, a wise fool is the foolishest fool of all ! "

" We will enjoy this phase of the subject later," said Mr. Morris, shaking a reproving finger at the doctor. " At present we are in need of more light."

" I think I can help you to it ! " said Mr. Draper, with a brisk nod of the head. " I was honored with Miss Percy's confidence from the first ; but even before that, another lady wrote to me of her troubles, and summoned me from the other side of the water to her aid. Let me also say that I am not a rich man. To assist Miss Gower, I was com- pelled to leave my business, and the money I used comes from the sale of some little property I was compelled to dispose of in pieces ; and that at the present moment I am still waiting for the money that was to have been sent me months ago. I never entered a gambling house in my life. I mention these trifles to account for several little unhap- pinesses in my Cypressville history. Let me add, that I have crossed and recrossed the ocean several times in this little business ; neglecting my affairs, to return and set them right, and so on ! "

He nodded gayly to Miss Gower, then continued :

" Originally, it was my belief that Miss Gower was being cheated out of money that rightly belonged to her. In my endeavors to discover the truth of the report, I gained some knowledge of the inner life of Mr. Addison, and for a while used it to some purpose in restraining his malice. I visited him again and again, and let me confess that, despite his wickedness, I felt more pity than anger, for it was not long before I discovered that he was insane, hopelessly insane !—a helpless automaton, in the hands of a cunning servant. On certain sides he was unusually bright, almost brilliant ; on others a wreck ! A madhouse was his proper place, and I once urged this fact on his servant, but I was laughed at for my pains, and gained the reputation of being a cunning plotter. My belief as to the money turned out to be wrong, and under the circumstances nothing was to be done. I did not know of the plot that was being hatched against Miss Gower, and so I advised patience and cheerfulness."

"Did she not visit you very much ?" asked the doctor, severely.

"She visited me and I visited her whenever we felt like it !" answered Geoffrey cheerfully. "Just before the wretched business, she visited me at my house, and had a very interesting conversation on money matters, which fact, I am told, has very much puzzled the brain of the cunning Detective Sharpe. Thanks to Miss Percy, I finally heard something of the plot, and also, thanks to her, I was made acquainted with a secret entrance into the old house ; which I frequently made use of. From this use I learned that Mr. Addison's long yacht voyage was only a pretense to throw his creditors off their guard. For a year he knew that he had exhausted most of his resources, and for a year he endeavored to save himself by gambling

and by speculation. In his leisure moments he
visited his house, coming at night by boat and
entering it by a secret passage near the water.
Let me say it was a year of evil and excesses, and
that Mr. Addison's insanity was not improved by it.
By playing the part of spy, I was punished by wit-
nessing a scene that filled me with horror, and
which I can not even now think of without my blood
turning into ice. On a certain morning, hidden in
the library, I witnessed what you call the ' murder', and I there grappled with the man whom
you call the ' murderer '! I had listened to a
long conversation wherein a certain paper was
mentioned, and the damnation of Miss Gower
finally completed, and then I witnessed the ' murder'! In my horror, I revealed my presence.
Max Newton rushed at me with a knife, and in
defending myself, I was wounded in the palm of
the hand, and, as the doctor shall see by and by,
the wound has not yet healed! I was still under
the influence of the horror, and made discretion the
better part of valor. I leaped through the open
library window, caught hold of the ivy with my
wounded hand, and reached the ground. The
blood flowed from the wound in a stream, and I
used my handkerchief to wipe it away. Having no
reason for concealment, I cast the blood-soaked
handkerchief away, and thus gave rigid science an
opportunity to draw its infallible conclusions, and
assist the noble cause of justice! Fearing pursuit,
and unmanned by what I had seen, I crept into the

bushes and there became unconscious. When my
senses returned, the horror returned with them, and
a curiosity was born that was greater than the
horror. Indifferent to my wound, I had a mania
to again glance in the room. My teeth chattered
and my limbs trembled, but I could not resist the
craving. I grasped the ivy, drew myself up to the
window sill, and peeped in. I loosened my grasp,
and fell half paralyzed, as a pistol shot blazed close
to my eyes. I had fallen to the ground, but I picked
myself up and ran away as quickly as I could.
When I was comparatively calm I sought Miss Percy, and we discussed the matter. It was my wild
opinion that we should inform justice at once ; it
was her more sensible conclusion that we should
wait until we had Miss Gower's defense in our
hands. It was finally decided that I should conceal myself till evening in Miss Gower's room, and
then boldly invade the house in the night in
search of a certain paper ; that is, Miss Percy was
to enter the house by the secret passage, and I was
to wait outside to give assistance in case of need.
It was not difficult to get into Miss Gower's room ;
the doctor and Captain Travers were away ; Mr.
Morris was sleeping in his own room. The difficulty was to keep Miss Gower quiet ; she insisted
on accompanying us, and even put on her bonnet,
fearing that we might give her the slip. She was
very nervous, very hysterical, and we agreed that
she should go with us. This conclusion reached
Miss Percy retired."

The doctor coughed, and shook his head ; Captain Travers frowned, and even Mr. Morris looked surprised.

Geoffrey Draper, however, paid no attention to these symptoms, but calmly continued his narrative:

" At the time agreed on, Miss Percy returned, and before setting out, we all took a glass of wine to cheer us. We had put opium in Miss Gower's glass to free ourselves from her, and when she was helpless, we set out and reached the house without trouble. Miss Percy disappeared, and I kept guard outside. Unfortunately, the enemy was bolder than I imagined. In the gathering gloom I saw several suspicious-looking objects stealthily approaching me. As I afterward learned, they were some of the crew from the yacht ; people who had been bought heart and soul by their master. I gave the warning whistle agreed on, and then attempted to escape ; but it was too late ! On all sides they rushed toward me. I fired my pistol at them, threw it away, and took to my heels. It was foggy, and I nearly fell into the well. I escaped this only to rush into the arms of the enemy. I was knocked down, in silence on their part, gagged, tied, and carried to the yacht, where I remained a prisoner until Miss Percy rescued me ! "

" To *my* way of thinking," said Mr. Morris, " it was a foolish expedition. It was not likely you would find the paper you were looking for. The murderer would have removed it from its hiding place ! "

" You are wrong," answered Mr. Draper, "and it was surely there on the evening when we looked for it ; for, immediately after the shot, it was necessary for Max Newton to leap on the yacht that touched at his place, and pretend that he had come up in it from the city."

"I had just found the door of the trap," said Miss Percy, " when I saw a ray of moonlight falling on a figure in the doorway. I thought it was Max Netwon, and, losing my wits, rushed into Captain Travers's arms."

" Had *I* been in your place," said the doctor, severely. " I should have fired at the murderer."

" But there was no murder ! " said Mr. Draper quietly.

These words caused the greatest excitement.

" Come, come, this is carrying it *too* far," said the doctor, frowning. " Perhaps," he said, with fine scorn, " the dead man is alive ! "

" I have not said so, doctor. He had squandered a fortune, he was deeply in debt, he was insane, and he hated the one woman who had resisted him ! With diabolical malice, he saved himself from exposure and revenged himself at the same time by *taking poison*, and with his own lips directing that a certain time after death—he had a horror of blood !—he should be shot in the head with a pistol he had formerly given to Miss Gower, but which was still in his possession ! "

" And which I delivered to Dr. Dubois," interrupted Miss Percy. " My fidelity was strongly

suspected at the time by Max Newton, and it was
he who gave me the pistol and the order to surrender it.   I obeyed, knowing that the doctor would
speak of it to his good friend Mr. Salors, otherwise
Detective Sharpe, and that the wise detective would
speak of it to Max Newton, and in this way save
the bad man's suspicion from deepening against
me ! "

"I heard all the details of the intended suicide
discussed by master and man as if it were the most
ordinary affair in life. I heard the insane man
give his orders as calmly as if he were only going
on a short journey ; and I saw the madman's passion in his eyes as he spoke of the evils that he was
bringing on an innocent woman ! "

The doctor indulged in a significant cough ; but
observing Miss Percy's contemptuous smile, he
cunningly pretended that he was struggling with a
temporary obstruction in his throat.

Mr. Draper continued :

" I saw the madman drink the poison as if it were
the most luxurious wine ; and when, after my senses
returned, and I peeped in the window, I saw Max
Newton fire the pistol bullet into the dead man's
head, holding the head on his knee, having previously poured blood on the floor, in obedience to
his master's orders that none of his own blood
should be spilled ! "

" If this is not enough," said Miss Percy, " I have
the honor of presenting for the doctor's considera-
tion a letter written by Mr. Addison just before his

death, and which was to have been delivered only after his victim's character was hopelessly ruined. He wished her to live and suffer, and it was to have reached her after she had been tried and condemned to the gallows. Will you read it, Mr. Draper?"

With the words she held out the paper that she had taken from the drugged Max Newton.

Mr. Draper tore open the sealed envelope, extracted a paper, and read:

" MY SWEETEST LOVE, ORIANA :

"I am tired of the world and intend to leave it ; but I am still determined you shall not forget me. I am going to kill myself, and allow the world to believe you are my murderer. But you must not hang ; you must live and think of me ! So, my love, I write this letter, which you will receive when the hangman's fingers are on your throat. It will save your life, and give you an opportunity to gauge my love by my hate ! You are penniless, blasted in name, a jail-bird ! I now free you. Cleanse the foulness I have thrown on you, if you can ! I hate the world and I hate you, my love ! Tell the hangman I die by my own hand, by poison. Farewell, my sweet, and remember, in your degradation,

" HUGO ADDISON."

"September 13, 18—."

" The scoundrel ! " hissed Captain Travers. Then he said, somewhat nervously, "I would like to ask who you are, Mr. Draper ? You see—that is—"

"Yes, who *are* you?" repeated the doctor, irritably.

"I am Oriana's brother, Geoffrey Draper Gower!"

"Ah, Dubois," said Mr. Morris, enjoying his friend's discomfiture, "it's a shame you can't share the laurels with the sleuth-hound Sharpe! Long live science!"

"I wish Miss Churchill were here to enjoy these developments," said Miss Percy, with a sigh.

"I received a telegram from her this morning," answered the humbled doctor. "Allow me to read it, that she may receive a portion of the attention now showered on me."

The doctor took a paper from his pocket and, with quiet malice, read as follows:

"DR. DUBOIS: I have left the city; but be easy. The mystery will be solved soon. *I* am on the track of the yacht *Oriana!*"

When Captain Travers departed for Europe he was accompanied by the wife whom he had recently married—a charming young lady, who has forsworn the use of laudanum even in sickness, and who bears a strong resemblance to Miss Gower.

Miss Percy traveled in the same vessel, and a certain "Geoffrey Draper" is very fond of sitting beside her and admiring the stars. Perhaps one day she may forget her objections to marriage, and become a very excellent and loving wife.

From a newspaper of a later date we extract the following item:

"In a recent storm a great many vessels were wrecked, and among them a once-famous yacht called the *Oriana*. A returned vessel reports having seen the ill-starred yacht founder in mid-ocean, carrying down with it, in one fell swoop, all its occupants. On account of the high seas, assistance was impossible, and so both vessel and crew were swallowed up by the devastating elements. On the following morning a man was seen, clutching a spar. He was rescued, but died soon after. The body was recognized as that of Max Newton, who was connected with a tragedy which is already a medico-legal classic, and which future moralists will extensively use to point a moral and adorn a tale!"

THE END.

AS IT WAS WRITTEN.

A Jewish Musician's Story.

BY SIDNEY LUSKA.

1 VOLUME 16MO. EXTRA CLOTH. PRICE, - - $1.00.

OPINIONS OF THE PRESS.

"'AS IT WAS WRITTEN' is certainly a work of no common sort. It is full of passion and virile struggle, and will make its mark."—GEORGE CARY EGGLESTON.

"Its intensity, picturesqueness and exciting narration are in sharp contrast with the works of our analytic novelists."—E. C. STEDMAN.

"It is safe to say that few readers who have perused the first chapter, will be content to lay the book down without finishing it."—*Christian Union*, New York.

"The working out of so strange and abnormal a plot without any descent into mere grotesqueness is a triumph of art."—*New York Tribune.*

"It is vivid without floridness, dreamy without sentiment, exciting without being sensational."—*The Critic*, New York.

"We can earnestly advise all readers who care for a novel showing individuality, power and thought, to read AS IT WAS WRITTEN."—*Brooklyn Union.*

"A capital novel. . . . It cannot fail to impress itself as an able and moving dramatic effort."—*New York Times.*

"Of all the novels that have come to us this season, AS IT WAS WRITTEN seems the most likely to take a permanent place in literature. We hope to hear from Sidney Luska again."—*Yale Courant.*

"We have seen no book of late years to which the term absorbing in interest could more appropriately be applied."—*Boston Herald.*

"It stands apart from the average novel, soon invites attention and then rivets it. . . . Will doubtless be extensively read."—*New York Telegram.*

CASSELL & COMPANY, Limited,

739 and 741 Broadway, New York.

AT LOVE'S EXTREMES.

BY MAURICE THOMPSON,

Author of "A TALLAHASSE GIRL," "SONGS OF FAIR WEATHER," etc., etc.

1 Vol., 12mo. Cloth. Price, $1.00.

The scene of the story is laid in the mountains of Alabama ; it is a thoroughly American tale, as strong as it is picturesque.

The story is a very strong one, with picturesque sketching, effective dramatic situations, and most admirable character drawing.—*Boston Home Journal.*

Crisp and fresh in style, and the story is told with animation.—*Brooklyn Daily Times.*

The attractive setting, the general color, and the excellence of parts of the action make the novel a very strong one.—*Boston Globe.*

It is bright with descriptions of scenes, and spicy with mountaineer dialect. . . . The style is charming, and this new work of fiction will be read widely and with pleasure.—*St. Louis Globe Democrat.*

A delightful story, elegantly designed, and told in the most interesting manner.—*Press, Albany.*

The author has blended the beautiful and romantic in graceful thought which charms and entertains the reader.—*Southern Agriculturist.*

CASSELL & COMPANY, Limited,

739 and 741 Broadway, New York.

THE
WORLD'S WORKERS.

A SERIES OF

TERSELY WRITTEN BIOGRAPHIES OF THOSE WHOSE LIVES WERE FILLED WITH NOBLE AND INSPIRING EXAMPLES.

Each Volume Contains a Portrait Frontispiece.

12mo., ORNAMENTED CLOTH, 128 PAGES. PRICE PER VOLUME, 50 CENTS.

Sold Separately or in Sets.

CASSELL & COMPANY, Limited,
739 & 741 Broadway, New York.

www.ingramcontent.com/pod-product-compliance
Lightning Source LLC
Chambersburg PA
CBHW020055030726
47498CB00006B/1801